STO

FRIENDS
OF ACPL

W9-BAT-574

WHO NEEDS ESPIE SANCHEZ?

Also by Terry Dunnahoo
This Is Espie Sanchez
Who Cares About Espie Sanchez?

WHO NEEDS ESPIE SANCHEZ?

by Terry Dunnahoo

E. P. Dutton   *New York*

Copyright © 1977 by Terry Dunnahoo

All rights reserved. No part of this publication may be
reproduced or transmitted in any form or by any means,
electronic or mechanical, including photocopy, recording,
or any information storage and retrieval system now
known or to be invented, without permission in writing
from the publisher, except by a reviewer who wishes to
quote brief passages in connection with a review written
for inclusion in a magazine, newspaper, or broadcast.

Library of Congress Cataloging in Publication Data

Dunnahoo, Terry.   Who needs Espie Sanchez?

SUMMARY: Espie Sanchez's curiosity is aroused by a
young wealthy girl who befriends her after both are
involved in a tragic traffic accident.

[1. Alcoholics—Fiction. 2. Alcoholism—Fiction.
3. Mexican Americans—Fiction] I. Title.
PZ7.D92172Wj [Fic] 77-7147 ISBN: 0-525-42704-X

Published in the United States by E. P. Dutton, a Division
of Sequoia-Elsevier Publishing Company, Inc., New York

Published simultaneously in Canada by Clarke,
Irwin & Company Limited, Toronto and Vancouver

Editor: Ann Durell   Designer: Laurel Danowitz
Printed in the U.S.A.   First Edition
10 9 8 7 6 5 4 3 2 1

To my sister Annette,
with love

1975337

CHAPTER 1

Mr. Harlan shouted above the noise in the tunnel-like warehouse. "This float won't be ready for the parade."

Espie Sanchez pressed a carnation petal on the float Los Angeles had entered in the Tournament of Roses Pageant and shouted back at him, "My fingers won't work anymore. They're too cold."

"Make them work or this thing won't roll down Colorado Boulevard tomorrow," the man said. He took a handful of petals and slapped them on the float so fast, Espie leaned closer to make sure he had put them on straight.

"You don't have frostbite," she said.

Mr. Harlan smiled and picked up the bucket beside her. "I'll get more glue."

Espie wished she could go for it. Her whole body was numb with cold, and after four hours of kneeling on the cement floor she thought her knees might never straighten up. "Who got us in this mess?" she asked Denise Manning, her roommate in Mrs. Garcia's foster home.

Denise laughed and leaned back on her heels. "You did. When Officer Parks told us she knew a great way for the

Explorers to earn money, you asked how. She said help trim the floats for the Rose Parade, and you said great."

"Well, you all agreed with me." Espie winced. She rubbed her hands and put them under her armpits to warm them. She and Denise were inches away from each other and only a couple of feet from Rosemary Freeman, who was pulling petals off carnations, but they had to shout to make themselves heard over the noise that filled the block-long building.

Mr. Harlan came back with the glue. "The boss says half this crew can go to the chow line."

Espie jumped up. Her legs buckled, and she fell against Mr. Harlan. "Sorry," she said.

"Better me than the float," he told her.

He moved away from the Los Angeles float, and Espie and twenty other kids followed in single file. At one point they had to ease their bodies sideways between floats. Espie felt crammed by wall-to-wall flowers, and wall-to-wall people.

After Espie and Denise got a hamburger and hot chocolate on the chow line, they found a couple of empty chairs at the end of the food table. Espie took a sip of her drink. The hot chocolate warmed her insides. She bit into her hamburger and began to feel better.

"I saw the parade last year. I hitched a ride and camped out with a bunch of kids I met."

Denise said, "I used to see it every New Year's with my folks, but I haven't seen it since. . . . Since I went to live with Mrs. Garcia."

Denise had trouble saying her parents were dead. To Espie, dead was bad, but it beat having your father desert you and hearing your mother tell the cops she didn't want you.

2

Denise finished her hamburger. "I have to go to the head. Want me to wait for you?"

"I'll go later," Espie told her.

As soon as Denise stood up, a guy sat beside Espie. "Hi, I'm Hank. What float you working on?"

"The one from Los Angeles," she said. He was a nice-looking guy if you liked blonds. Espie sipped her hot chocolate.

"What's your name?"

"Espie Sanchez."

"What group you with?" Hank asked just before he bit off half his hamburger.

"The L.E.E.G.s."

Hank laughed. Half-chewed food stuck to his teeth and lips. "Yeah, and I'm with the arms."

Espie crushed her empty cup. "The letters stand for Law Enforcement Explorer Group."

Hank looked serious. "You work with the cops?" Espie nodded. She still wasn't used to the idea that Espie Sanchez was a mini-pig. "What do you do?" Hank asked.

"Lots of things. Take reports, look for evidence, do search-and-rescue."

"No kidding? How long you been one of these L.E.E.G.s?"

"I graduated from the police academy three weeks ago. They put me through brain-and-body torture for nine Saturdays to see if I could handle myself." She leaned back and hooked her thumbs in the belt loops of her jeans. "I can handle myself," she said.

Hank smiled. "I bet you can. Why'd you join?"

Espie shrugged and stood up. "I have to get back to the float."

She threw her empty cup and plate into the trash con-

3

tainer and started for the door that led to the head. No use telling him she joined the Explorers so she could get out of Mrs. Garcia's house after the guy at juvenile court put her there in June for running away from home. Or that until she joined, she was as much a prisoner in the foster home as she would have been in juvey.

The Academy had been rough, but the day after she graduated, she went to Disneyland. That had been something she'd wanted for a long time. Now she was working on the float to earn money for other trips. This wasn't the greatest way to spend New Year's Eve, but it was better than sitting with Mrs. Garcia or watching her mother booze herself up until she passed out on the couch the way she did last year.

The food had warmed her, but she shivered as she walked outside to the portable toilets in back of the building. She didn't see Denise, and after ten minutes of waiting in line, Espie was ready to get back to work.

A woman at the door glanced at the button on Espie's sweater and let her in. Every float crew wore a color-coded button so staff members knew where everybody belonged. Espie had stopped to watch a crew do patch-up work when a man in a dark blue jacket like the one Mr. Harlan wore looked at her button. "Los Angeles float, huh?" Espie nodded. His name tag said PILLER. "You going to let these guys beat you?"

"Nobody beats me," Espie said.

"Your float's way behind." When she didn't move he asked, "You staying with us until the parade?"

Espie shook her head. "I have to leave at nine. The girl I came with has to get the car back so her father can go to work."

The man looked at his watch as Espie moved away. "You've only got two hours. And you won't get back to your float if you go that way. Los Angeles is over here. Come on, I'll show you."

Espie walked behind him, glad to follow the dark blue jacket. She felt crammed into a big box of flowers. "Ever think of getting a larger building or fewer floats?" she asked as the man led her around the floats and people.

"We've thought of both, but this is the way it always ends up."

When they reached the L.A. float, Denise was back at work, and the half of the crew who hadn't eaten was gone. "We don't have all our people," Espie said.

Mr. Piller said, "They'll be back. Here, let me show you a fast way to put on those petals." He brushed glue on the side of the float and plastered petals on as fast as Mr. Harlan had done it.

Espie said, "Let me see you do that again." The man did it again. "Your hands moved so fast I didn't see how you keep both of them going without getting them in each other's way." Rosemary had stopped pulling petals off the flowers, and she and Denise were watching Espie.

Mr. Piller gave Espie the glue brush. "I've been doing this twenty years. I know a con when I see one."

Rosemary and Denise cracked up, and Espie shrugged. "You can't blame me for trying."

Mr. Piller laughed. "Keep at it. It'll be ready on time. Somehow floats always are." He got a call on his walkie-talkie and hurried away.

Espie went back to glueing. The rest of the crew straggled back. Her fingers began to freeze up on her again. She was trying to warm them when a woman walked slowly past her. Espie saw a JUDGE badge. She told Denise and Rosemary, "Hey, maybe we'll win a prize. I've never won anything."

Rosemary said, "The float might win, not you."

5

Espie said, "Well, I'm working on it, aren't I?"

Denise said, "Hundreds of people worked on this thing."

Espie put on more petals. "But this is the part that's going to help win the prize."

She saw Mr. Harlan check the back of the float, then walk toward the front. When he reached them, Espie said, "Mr. Harlan, will you show me how you put on these petals again? You must be the fastest petal-paster in the world."

Mr. Harlan smiled and put on several rows of carnation petals. Espie said, "Let me see you do that again. Your hands moved so fast I didn't see how you keep both of them going without getting them in each other's way." Mr. Harlan did it again. Espie saw Denise and Rosemary giggle.

Mr. Harlan was still working when music from the loudspeaker stopped and a voice said, "Ladies and gentlemen, we have a finished float."

Espie heard shouts behind her. "We are . . . number one! We are . . . number one!"

Mr. Harlan gave Espie the petals he was holding. "I have to get over there."

Denise told Espie, "If you get enough staff members to put on your petals, we could be number two."

Espie shrugged. "What's so big deal about being number one?" she said. She brushed glue on the float. Damn it. She'd never been number one in anything.

Twenty minutes later the music was interrupted again, and a voice said, "Ladies and gentlemen, a second float has been completed." A girl on the other side of the Los Angeles float shouted, "We won't be last. We won't be last." Other kids joined her. There were nine L.E.E.G.s working on the float. The rest of the crew was from a couple of schools in L.A., and within minutes everybody was yelling, "We won't be last."

Espie shouted at Rosemary, "What time is it?"

Rosemary glanced at her watch. "A quarter to nine."

Denise said, "We'd better find Mr. Harlan and tell him we have to leave."

Espie looked past her. "Here he comes."

Three boys and three girls followed close behind him. "The schedule says three of you Explorers have to go at nine, so I brought more help."

Espie said, "I figured it would take six regular people to replace three L.E.E.G.s."

Rosemary said, "Let's go. My father'll kill me if I'm late." They said good-bye to Mr. Harlan and waved to the rest of the crew. When Espie reached the back of the float, she grabbed a rose and shoved it under her sweater.

There were hundreds of cars and thousands of people outside. Rosemary moaned, "We'll never get out of here."

Denise said, "Sure we will. This crowd is here for the night. Once we clear the area we'll be going against the traffic."

Espie opened the back door and got in behind Rosemary while Denise sat in front. The car crawled along. Espie took the rose from under her sweater, and Denise said, "I can still smell those flowers."

Espie sniffed the rose. "This what you smell?"

Denise turned. "When did you take that?"

"On the way out. I wanted to see how alert Mr. Harlan's guards were. They'd make lousy Explorers." She held the flower to her nose and smelled it again. "I'm going to give it to Mrs. Garcia."

Denise said, "She won't take a stolen flower."

Espie looked at Denise. "Who's going to tell her it's stolen?"

Denise turned forward in her seat. "Not me," she said.

Espie watched the unbroken line of headlights on the other side of the street. She knew Denise wouldn't fink.

Rosemary picked up speed, and within minutes they were on the freeway doing fifty-five. Espie said, "I wish I could see the parade."

Rosemary told her. "Me too, but I wouldn't want to wait all night in the cold."

Espie said, "It's not bad. You sing and talk. Some of the kids play guitars and dance. It's like a party."

Rosemary said, "A cold party."

Espie remembered how cold she'd been the year before and how cold she'd been decorating the float. "Yeah, a cold party."

Rosemary took the Figueroa Street off-ramp and headed east. She was halfway through the intersection at Figueroa and Avenue 50 when Espie saw the headlights. "Watch out," she yelled. Lights blinded her. Steel hit steel and silenced Denise's screams.

CHAPTER 2

"This one's dead."

Espie heard the words through a jumble of voices, footsteps, and a distant siren.

Red and yellow lights flashed across her eyelids. She forced them open, but she couldn't get her mouth to work. She tried to move.

The man beside her said, "Everything's under control. Lie still." He held her right eyelid, and put a light to her eye, then did the same to her left one. "My name's Pete," he said. His fingers moved quickly from one side of her head to the other. "That hurt?" he asked. Espie shook her head.

Her brain began to clear. "Who's dead?" she asked.

Pete's finger pressed her neck. "This hurt?"

Espie said, "Is Denise dead?"

"Our only fatality is male."

"Where's Denise?" she asked, and when Pete didn't answer, she screamed Denise's name. But Denise didn't answer, and Espie tried to get up.

Pete held her down. She saw Rosemary run toward her.

"You okay?" Rosemary asked as she fell on her knees beside Espie. Pete was pressing on her ribs and still asking if his poking was hurting her.

Espie kept shaking her head. She asked Rosemary, "How's Denise?"

"They just got her out of the car. She's banged up pretty bad."

"She going to be okay?"

"I don't know. She's unconscious."

Pete said, "You can sit up." He helped her. "Have any pain now?"

"No."

The siren hushed to a whisper as a police car stopped near the ambulance. Another police car and ambulance stood several yards away. Espie stood up. Her world spun, then stopped. "Where's Denise?" she asked Pete.

"Over here."

They passed something covered with a blanket. A policeman asked a girl, "How much liquor did you have?"

The girl said, "I've only had a couple of Cokes."

"Then why can't you walk a straight line?"

Espie didn't hear the answer. She saw a guy bent over Denise. Another one was talking into a mike.

"We have a female, approximately fifteen years . . ."

"Sixteen," Espie told him.

The man ignored her. "Unconscious, possible lumbar spinal injury. Skin color normal, pupils dilated, reactive. Blood pressure 100 over 60, pulse 115 to 120, respiration 20."

The voice from the radio sounded sure and urgent. "Start I.V. 5 percent dextrose with half normal saline. Place on backboard, sandbag the neck, and transport to hospital, Code 3."

10

Espie watched the men work on Denise. Finally, Pete said, "Miller, this one goes with you. We'll take the body." Espie winced at the word.

"Vitals normal?" Miller asked, and Pete nodded. Miller turned to Espie. "Sit over there." He pointed to the seat at the back of the ambulance. Espie stepped up. "Move it," he said. "And tie the seat belt."

Espie glared at him. They sure stopped being nice when they found out you were okay. She sat down, and the men pushed in the gurney. Miller hopped up, and the other attendant closed the door. Before he reached the front of the ambulance, Miller had put small bags on each side of Denise's neck. The motor started, the siren came alive, and Miller pulled a bottle and tubes from a cabinet. He stuck a needle in Denise's arm.

"What are you doing to her?" Espie asked.

Miller ignored her. She heard the driver say, "Bay station, this is unit seven-two, we have stat, ident, booth C, E.T.A. ten minutes."

"Ten-four, unit seven-two," the radio answered.

Espie didn't know exactly what they were talking about. She saw the liquid bubble in the bottle connected to Denise's arm. Miller was taking her blood pressure again.

Espie said, "She's going to be okay, isn't she? I mean, she's not even bleeding anymore."

Miller took the stethoscope from his ears and let it hang around his neck. He wrote down some figures, then looked up. "She's holding steady. What's her name?"

"Denise Manning." The driver turned a corner, and Espie held on to the seat.

"What's her phone number?" Espie told him. "Think her folks are home?"

"We live with a foster mother—Mrs. Garcia." His body

11

moved with the ambulance, but even with a seat belt Espie had trouble holding hers steady as the ambulance weaved in and out of traffic.

"You going to call Mrs. Garcia?"

"They'll do it at the hospital. They need permission to work on a juvenile."

The ambulance turned and slowed. The siren died. The driver stopped, shifted, and backed up. Miller pushed the doors open and jumped out. A nurse helped him pull the gurney. Before Espie got out, they were rolling it down the platform.

The driver asked her, "You okay?" Espie nodded. "Let's go then."

Espie saw the nurse steady the bottle that was still connected to Denise by tubes. The doors opened automatically, and they pushed Denise past the red sign that said EMERGENCY ADMITTING ROOM.

Miller said, "We're unit seven-two."

A doctor grabbed the front of the gurney and pulled it into a room. Miller and the nurse went in. The door closed in front of Espie. "Hey, let me in," she shouted. She banged the door. Her fists rattled the plastic sign that read ROOM C.

The driver told her, "You can't go in there."

"Miller said he'd call Mrs. Garcia. I have to talk to her."

There was movement and noise everywhere—wheelchairs, shuffling bodies, nurses, and calls and commands crackling over the loudspeakers. A nurse approached them. Her name tag said VICKERS. The driver told her, "I'm Steve Wade, unit seven-two. Here's the patient's vital signs." The woman glanced at the paper he handed her.

Espie saw three phones on the wall. "I have to call Mrs. Garcia."

The nurse said, "They're doing that right now."

Espie started for the phones. "I have to talk to her."

The nurse grabbed her arm. "We'll let you call in a minute," she said.

Miller came out of Room C with his gurney. Espie asked, "How's Denise?"

"They're working on her," he said. He asked the nurse, "You get the vitals on this one?" He pointed to Espie, and the nurse nodded. "Okay, sign here," he said.

The nurse wrote her name, and Miller told Espie, "Listen, they're really trying in there." He walked away, the doors opened automatically, and he and Wade stepped out.

The nurse said, "I'll check you over for the doctor, then you can make your call." She picked up a clipboard. "How tall are you?"

"Five feet two."

"How much do you weigh?"

"Ninety-two pounds."

Vickers put a thermometer in Espie's mouth and wrapped the blood-pressure gauge around her arm. Espie watched the closed door on Room C. A woman walked past it with a crying baby in her arms. She asked a nurse behind the desk, "When you going to give me something for my baby?"

The nurse said, "The doctors are all busy right now."

The woman sat down beside a man holding an ice bag over his eye. "Hey, lady, shut that kid up. My head's killing me." The woman unbuttoned her dress and put a breast in the baby's mouth.

Espie mumbled, "What's in that room?" and grabbed the thermometer before it slipped out of her mouth.

Vickers said, "Everything that keeps people breathing. I've even seen them bring patients back to life in there." She took the thermometer from Espie's mouth and read it.

"You can make your call now, then sit over there, and I'll clean up those lacerations for the doctor."

Espie hurried to one of the phones and dialed Mrs. Garcia's number. She picked it up on the first ring. "Hello."

"I'm okay and they're taking care of Denise," Espie said quickly, trying to keep her voice steady.

"They say Denise is hurt bad."

"Yeah, but they'll . . ." The door of Room C opened, and a nurse rolled a bed out. Two doctors and another nurse hurried behind it. Espie dropped the phone and ran. "Where you taking her?" she asked. Denise's blond hair was damp and matted. Her face, colorless above the red blanket that covered her, bore a mask of pain. Nobody even looked at Espie. "Where you going?" she shouted, and clenched the nurse's arm.

"Neurosurgery," the woman said. She pulled her arm away just before the doors closed behind her.

Espie stared through the glass doors at their receding backs, then remembered Mrs. Garcia. She heard the woman's shouts before she reached the phone. "Espie, what is happening? Espie?"

Espie picked up the receiver that hung from the wall. "They just took Denise to Neurosurgery."

"They tell me that word, but I no understand what it means. I just tell them to take care of her."

Espie saw a couple of policemen walk in and go to the desk. She recognized one as the cop who had questioned the girl beside the blanket-covered body. Espie's head began to ache. She didn't want to be alone anymore. "Call Carlos and ask him to bring you to the hospital," she told Mrs. Garcia.

"They tell me I must come for you, so I call him. But he must work to midnight. Then he come."

The clock on the wall said eleven fifteen. "I'll be in the

emergency room. If they release me before you get here, I'll go to Neurosurgery."

"Espie, you are all right? I am worried about you too."

"I'm fine, honest."

Mrs. Garcia said, "Then I go pray for Denise."

Espie hung up. The cops approached her. One of them said, "I'm Officer Newman, and this is my partner, Officer Berrigan. The nurse says your friend is in Neurosurgery." Espie nodded. "Anybody coming for you?"

"Mrs. Garcia. Denise and I live with her."

Officer Newman said, "Rosemary told us."

"Where is Rosemary?"

"Her folks picked her up at the scene," Officer Berrigan said. He pulled out his notebook and flipped the pages until he found a blank one. "What's your full name?" he asked.

"Esperanza Sanchez."

"What's your address?" She told him, and he wrote it down. "Okay, Esperanza, tell us what happened."

"All I know is we were going through the intersection at Figueroa and Avenue 50 when I saw headlights coming at us. I heard the crash. Next thing I remember, I'm in the street with some guy telling me everything's under control."

"Where were you sitting in the car?" Berrigan asked.

"Behind Rosemary. How come she didn't get hurt?"

Newman said, "The right side of your car took the impact of the crash. That trapped Denise, but Rosemary was able to get out the driver's door."

Berrigan asked, "Do you remember opening the door beside you?"

Espie shook her head. "I didn't touch it." Her mind raced to the crash. "Hey, wait. The door opened, and I fell out. That's right. I fell out."

15

"And the next thing you remember is the ambulance attendant working over you?" Berrigan said. Espie nodded. The officer was writing it all down.

Espie asked, "How many people in the other car?"

"Two. The driver was dead at the scene, a kid named Alex Bourne. The passenger was thrown from the car, but she's okay. She went home with her parents."

"I fall out, and I'm stuck here. She gets thrown out, and she's home."

Newman said, "That's what happens sometimes."

"What's the girl's name?"

Berrigan flipped the notebook pages. "Allison Summers."

Espie didn't recognize the name. Berrigan closed his notebook. "Thanks, Esperanza. We'll go see if we can talk to Denise."

"She's still unconscious."

"They told us at the desk she regained consciousness in there," Newman said. He pointed toward Room C.

"She did?" Espie hurried to Nurse Vickers. "They say Denise came to before she went to Neurosurgery."

Vickers talked to the nurse behind the desk. The woman nodded. Espie said, "Hey, that's great."

Vickers smiled and picked up a tray. "Come on, I'll clean you up so you'll be ready for discharge if we ever get a doctor to release you."

More people had been moving in and out of the room since Espie had arrived. Some New Year's Eve! A changing scene of sick, bleeding, broken people. The woman with the baby was gone, but the man with the ice bag was still there beside a man with a hacking cough.

"Is it always like this?" Espie asked.

Vickers put an alcohol-soaked cotton swab on a cut over

16

Espie's left eye. She winced. "New Year's Eve is always bad."

Espie glanced at the clock. A quarter to twelve. Mrs. Garcia and Carlos should be there by twelve thirty.

Vickers treated the scratches on the side of Espie's face and behind her left ear. Her sweater and jeans had protected her arms and legs. When the nurse finished, she said, "Sit over there until we call your name."

"How long do I have to wait?"

"That depends how many first-class emergencies we get. The doctors see those first."

"Can't I go see how Denise is?"

"You have to wait for a doctor. Besides, you can't leave this room until there's an adult to sign for you."

"That won't be until twelve thirty."

"It'll probably be that long before a doctor has time to sign your release," Vickers said. A patient called her, and she hurried away.

Espie leaned against the wall while her eyes measured the distance between her and the doors. They opened and paramedics ran in with a gurney. "We're unit five-eight," one of them said and headed for Room C as horns and sirens blared outside. Shouts of "Happy New Year" came over the loudspeaker. Espie slipped out into the hall.

She hurried to a group of signs and stopped just long enough to get directions to Neurosurgery. An arrow pointed to the right, and she ran past several people gathered around a coffee machine. They stared at her, and she slowed to a walk. She didn't want anybody asking her where she was going.

The nurse behind the desk looked up when Espie entered the room. "I want to see Denise Manning," she said.

"Denise is undergoing tests."

"How long will it take?"

"I don't know."

"Can't you go find out?"

The phone rang, and the nurse picked it up. "Neuro-surgery," she said and listened. She looked at Espie. "All right. I'll take care of it right away." She put down the receiver. "Okay, Espie, back to the emergency room."

Espie put her thumbs in the belt loops of her jeans and sat down. "You can't make me go."

The nurse dialed a number, talked into the receiver, then hung it up. Within minutes a guard came in. "Okay, out," he said.

Espie said, "I'm not a prisoner. I'm a patient."

"I know, and Emergency wants its patient back."

Espie glared at him, then stood up. Even on her feet she barely reached his shoulders. "You going to use hand-cuffs?" she asked.

The guard grinned. "Let's go."

Espie walked through the halls beside him. People stared at them. "Feel like a super jock?" she asked when they reached the emergency room. The doors opened, and she went in. The guard waved. Espie pushed her hair back and strolled away.

It was twelve twenty when Mrs. Garcia and Carlos came. Espie saw them before they saw her, and she hur-ried to them. Mrs. Garcia put her arms around her. "Espie, you are all right?" The woman held her so tightly, Espie pushed her away.

"I told you I was."

Carlos asked, "How's Denise?" His voice sounded tired. His black hair looked like it had been combed with his fingers instead of the brush he always kept in his back pocket.

"They're giving her tests."

18

Mrs. Garcia said, "Come, we go see her."

"I tried that," Espie said, and explained what had happened.

Carlos asked, "How long you going to be here?"

Espie pointed to the people sitting in the rows of chairs. "Probably until Easter."

Mrs. Garcia took a step toward the door. "I must see Denise."

Carlos told Espie, "I'll go with her."

"Okay, but hurry back."

Through the doors, Espie saw Carlos's slim body move ahead of Mrs. Garcia's heavy one. He stopped and adjusted his steps to hers. They turned a corner, and Espie began to pace the emergency room. One o'clock. One thirty. At a quarter to two Mrs. Garcia and Carlos came back.

"How is she?" Espie asked.

Mrs. Garcia said, "They tell me . . ." She stopped.

Espie looked at Carlos. "Maybe she won't be able to walk," he said.

"Ever?" Espie asked, and Mrs. Garcia's sobs answered the question.

CHAPTER 3

Espie had met Carlos Medina eight months ago, the day after she went to live with Mrs. Garcia. For a while Espie had a crush on him. He was part of the reason she worked to become an Explorer. But that feeling had passed, and now she thought of him as a friend who leveled with her.

"Why can't Denise walk?" she asked him, but Mrs. Garcia answered.

"There is something wrong in her spine."

Carlos said, "They've got her in traction. She's going to be in this place a long time."

Espie had learned first aid at the police academy, but the instructor only taught recruits how to take care of an injured person until help arrived. There hadn't been lessons about traction or spinal injury. But Carlos had taken a course at County General as part of the Explorer program, and when he finished explaining what traction was, Espie pictured Denise on her back unable to move.

"How does she feel?" Espie asked.

Mrs. Garcia said, "She is sleeping, so we cannot talk to her."

"Then how come you took so long?"

Carlos said, "We had to wait for the doctors to finish running the tests."

They sat down and talked about the accident and about Denise until they fell silent, tired of talking and tired of waiting.

It was almost three before a doctor signed Espie's release. She told him, "People get out of jail faster than they get out of here."

The doctor looked at her through bloodshot eyes. "If you guarantee that, I'll take up robbing little old ladies." A nurse called him, and he said to Mrs. Garcia, "I'm sorry it took so long." And before she could say anything, he disappeared into Room B, his shoulders slumped as though they would never straighten up again.

When they got outside, Carlos said, "I'll get the car and come back for you." He jogged across the deserted driveway, and Espie walked slowly beside Mrs. Garcia to a bench at a bus stop. Espie's teeth chattered from the cold. A man staggered toward them. "Happy New Year," he said. She shivered and thought of the thousands of people lining the streets of Pasadena waiting in the cold to see the parade.

She remembered the rose she had taken from the float. The flower must have fallen out of the car with her and gotten crushed at the corner of Figueroa and Avenue 50. "I had a rose for you," she told Mrs. Garcia. "But I lost it."

Mrs. Garcia touched her hand. "You are a good girl."

Nobody had told her that until she moved in with Mrs. Garcia, and Espie wondered if she'd ever get used to hearing it.

Carlos drove up in his old Chevy, and Espie got in the back while Mrs. Garcia struggled into the front seat. Espie shivered, both from the cold and from being in a car again so soon after the crash. Fifteen minutes later Carlos stopped in front of a wood frame house off Daly Street. "I won't be able to take you to the hospital tomorrow—I mean today. I have to work from noon until eight," he said.

Mrs. Garcia opened the door. "We will take the bus. It is nice you take me this time."

She got out, and Espie followed her. "Thanks, Carlos. I'll call you and let you know how Denise is."

She closed the door and walked up the sidewalk behind Mrs. Garcia. Carlos didn't leave until they were in the house.

It seemed as cold inside as it was outside. Mrs. Garcia said, "I will put on the heat." Espie stared at her. Mrs. Garcia never left the gas heater on all night because it cost so much to run. "The night is almost finished, and it is good you be warm after the accident." She turned the handle on the floor heater and started for her room. "We go to Mass at eleven o'clock instead of eight so you can sleep more."

Espie hadn't been to Mass on New Year's Day since her father left home three years ago when she was twelve. Her mother was always strung out that day, and Espie had just skipped Mass. But she knew there was no skipping Mass on a holy day of obligation as long as she lived with Mrs. Garcia. She felt the warmth from the heater. "That's a good idea," she said, as though she really didn't mind going to church.

She switched on the light in her room. Denise's uniform was still on her bed. She always hung it up when she took it off, but she had worked the desk at the Northeast Police Station before going to Pasadena to help decorate the float, and she had changed to her jeans only minutes before Rosemary picked them up. Espie got a couple of hangers

22

and put the navy-blue skirt and vest on one and the white blouse on the other, then put them in the closet. It would be a long time before Denise wore her uniform again. Espie stared at it—if she wore it again.

She pulled the blankets back and got into bed, too tired to undress. But every time she dozed, headlights coming at her and the crash of steel startled her awake. It was dawn before she slept undisturbed. Then Mrs. Garcia woke her for Mass.

"I call the hospital. They say Denise eat a good breakfast and is fine."

"That's great," Espie said, and stayed covered until Mrs. Garcia left the room. She didn't like Espie to sleep in her clothes, but Espie didn't mind. She used to do it all the time at home. It was easier to get out fast. Now she stretched and got up. She undressed and headed for the bathroom to take a shower, grateful that Mrs. Garcia had left the furnace on.

When she finished, Espie called Rosemary to tell her about Denise. But, although she told Rosemary about the tests and the traction, Espie didn't tell her Denise might not walk again. Somehow Espie couldn't bring herself to say it.

After Mass Espie and Mrs. Garcia ate lunch, then started for the bus stop. Several people were waiting when they reached the corner. "You wait long?" Mrs. Garcia asked a woman who sat on the bench at the curb.

"Ten minutes," the woman said, and Espie figured they had another ten minutes to wait. The bus picked them up at one thirty. Traffic was light, and even with frequent stops, they reached the hospital at two. They went in the front door instead of the emergency entrance, and Espie had to check the sign for directions. She pointed left. "Neurosurgery is this way."

Mrs. Garcia said, "Denise is not there. I tell you last night they move her to Ortho— Ortho— I no remember the word."

Espie couldn't remember, but she asked, as she looked at the list of wards, "Is it Orthopedic?"

"That is it."

"It's this way."

When they reached the ward, Espie asked for Denise. A nurse pointed past a row of beds. "She's in the last bed on the right."

Espie hurried toward the end of the room. People watched her from each side of the aisle. Some had an arm in traction, some had a leg. One girl had both legs raised on pulleys. Espie was almost beside Denise's bed when she turned. Her eyes looked tired and her face was black and blue, but her smile was instant. "It's about time you got here."

"We took a bus," Espie said, as though that explained everything.

Mrs. Garcia squeezed past Espie to Denise. "I am so afraid," the woman said, and hugged her a long time.

Espie asked, "How do you feel?"

"I hurt all over. They gave me some stuff, but I still feel the pain. And this thing they've got me in feels like a big heavy girdle."

"Can you move?"

"A little. I have to be able to get on the bedpan, don't I?" Denise made a face. "I'd hate to empty those things."

"I'd hate to use one," Espie said.

Mrs. Garcia looked from one to the other while they talked. "I am happy you are fine. The two of you," she said.

Denise reached for her hand and held it. "I'll be out of here in no time."

Mrs. Garcia didn't say anything about how long Denise might be in the hospital, and Espie didn't either. She asked Denise, "What do you remember about the accident?"

"Nothing except those lights coming at me. That's what I told the police when they talked to me last night or whenever it was they were here. I remember asking them how you and Rosemary were, and they said Rosemary went home, and you were okay."

Mrs. Garcia said, "Carlos bring me. I come see you, but you are sleeping after the tests so I go wait with Espie."

Espie said, "You can't get out of that emergency room unless you're dying. We didn't get home until three thirty."

Denise said, "Yeah, but you got out."

Espie pushed her hair back and tried to ignore the bitterness in Denise's voice. "Like you said, you'll be out of here in no time."

Denise asked, "What happened to the people in the other car?"

"The driver's dead," Espie said. She hadn't thought about the blanket-covered body since she'd passed it. For the first time, she realized the guy's family had to claim his body. She said quickly, "The girl was thrown out of the car, but she's okay. She went home with her folks."

"How come they came at us like that?"

"I think the guy was drunk."

"Know his name?" Denise asked slowly, and Espie decided Denise was also thinking for the first time that somebody besides them had been involved in the accident.

"Alex Bourne. The girl's name is Allison Summers."

"Hey, she's in my English class."

"I don't know her. What's she like?"

"I haven't seen her much. She's new. And she's absent a

lot. Failing, too. There's something bugging her." She shrugged. "Hey, the nurse told me the Los Angeles float won an award."

Espie put her thumbs in the belt loops of her jeans and leaned against the wall. "I told you the section I did would get an award." Denise laughed, then winced, her face covered with pain. Espie looked past her to the other beds. Some were flat like Denise's, but most of them had one end up. "Can't you put your bed up like those?"

"The nurse said maybe in a couple of days."

"What do you need from the house?" Mrs. Garcia asked Denise before they talked about how she and Espie would get back and forth from the hospital. They finally decided it was too dangerous to ride the bus at night. Unless Carlos brought them, Mrs. Garcia would have to visit alone during the day, and Espie would come with her on weekends.

Denise told Mrs. Garcia, "You sound like I'm going to be here forever."

"Not forever, but we must make plans for while you are here."

Espie said, "I can't come tomorrow. I have to work the desk from one to six. But I can come at night—and Thursday night."

Denise asked, "How about the Explorer meeting?"

"We cancelled it because of the holidays, remember?"

"Yeah, that's right."

Mrs. Garcia said, "Maybe Carlos drive us tomorrow night. I give him money for gas."

Espie realized the trips to the hospital would cut into Mrs. Garcia's budget. As a foster mother, she got money for taking care of Espie and Denise, but it didn't pay for everything, and Mrs. Garcia never asked for more. She just did a lot of sewing to make extra money.

A nurse approached the bed. She smiled at Mrs. Garcia and Espie and said to Denise, "Time for your pill."

Denise said, "I hope it's for pain."

The nurse gave her the pill and some water. "It is. The doctor ordered one every four hours."

Mrs. Garcia asked, "Can I talk to the doctor?"

"He isn't in now. But he'll be here for rounds tonight."

"I will not be here, and I want to talk to him about Denise."

The nurse took the small paper cup from Denise. "I'll have him call you, okay?"

"Thank you," Mrs. Garcia said, and the nurse walked away.

Mrs. Garcia turned back to Denise. "We must leave, or it will be dark when we get off the bus."

Espie said, "Yeah, I don't want to show up on the Northeast Division monthly crime sheet as a purse-snatch victim."

Denise said, "You don't even have a purse."

"Okay, then I don't want to show up as an assault-and-battery victim."

Denise said, "I know you have to go, but . . ." Tears filled her eyes, and Mrs. Garcia hugged her.

"I will come early tomorrow."

Denise brushed the tears away. "I'll . . . I'll be okay."

Espie said, "I'll call Carlos and Rosemary and ask them to come."

"Thanks." Denise brightened.

Espie started to walk away. Mrs. Garcia gave Denise another hug, and Espie turned back. "Hey, I'll come as soon as I can. Okay?"

Denise nodded. Espie waved and hurried out, sorry to leave Denise behind, but glad she wasn't the one who had to stay.

As soon as she got home, Espie called Rosemary, and she said she'd go see Denise the next day. They talked about the accident, and Espie told Rosemary that Allison Summers was in Denise's English class.

"Are they friends?"

"Denise doesn't even know her."

"How can she be in her class and not know her?" Rosemary went to Holy Trinity where almost everybody knew everybody.

"It's easy at Franklin Heights. Besides, she's new, and Denise said she's absent a lot." Espie leaned back in her chair and put her feet up on the phone table. "Hey, did you know our float won a prize?"

"Yeah, isn't that great?"

They talked about the float-decorating and the L.E.E.G.s until Mrs. Garcia told Espie to hang up so the phone wouldn't be busy when the doctor called.

At seven o'clock Mrs. Garcia went to her room to say the rosary in front of the statue of Our Lady of Guadalupe. Denise always said it with her when she was home, but Espie seldom did.

Espie went to her room. It was small with only two beds and one bureau, but it looked large and lonely without Denise. They had argued a few times since Espie had moved in, but Espie really liked Denise, and the empty room told her how much.

She heard Mrs. Garcia's Hail Marys. Espie figured she said the prayers out loud because she wanted Espie to hear them, but Denise insisted Mrs. Garcia had always prayed out loud. Espie didn't know how true that was, but she did know that every so often Mrs. Garcia's quiet voice got to her, and Espie went to kneel beside her. She did it now. She didn't know whether she believed in all those Hail Marys, but she hated to play Russian roulette with

God when Denise's chance of walking might depend on it.

The doctor called shortly before eight. After Mrs. Garcia hung up, she told Espie, "He say Denise will have less pain in a few days."

"What did he say about her back?"

"He still does not know how it will be."

"That's a bummer," Espie said.

"Maybe it will be fine. I pray it will be fine."

"Me too," Espie said.

She went to the phone and called Carlos to tell him how Denise was and to ask him to go see her the next day.

"I can't. I have to work from noon to eight again."

"How about Thursday night?"

"I'm working and I'm working twelve to eight Saturday and Sunday. You know Mr. Gomez—if he says work, I work, or he'll get somebody else."

"I know," Espie said. "Listen, I'll call tomorrow night and let you know how she is."

"Thanks," Carlos said.

Espie hung up and switched on the television. She turned it off a few minutes later and went back to the phone. She called Officer Mary Parks in the community-relations office, but she wasn't in. Parks would be on duty tomorrow when Espie worked the desk, and she'd tell her then about Denise. Espie dialed another number. Before she went to bed, she had called every L.E.G. in the Northeast Division and asked them to go see Denise. Denise would have done the same for her.

The next day, Mrs. Garcia took the bus to the hospital, and Espie got on one that would let her off a few blocks from the police station. It was a warm day, but Espie wore the coat Mrs. Garcia had made for her Christmas present. It hid her uniform. It wasn't that she was ashamed of it. It was just that she didn't like the stares or the name-calling she got when she wore it. Denise had told Espie she'd get used to being called piglet and mini-pig, but Espie wondered if she ever would.

When she got to the station, she waved to a couple of policemen she knew and walked up the steps behind a woman and a tall, slim girl. She smiled and held the door for Espie. They approached the desk together. The woman said, "I'm Mrs. Summers, and this is my daughter, Allison. We're supposed to see somebody in Juvenile."

Espie looked at the girl. Short black hair framed a face that was clean of make-up. Her green eyes, her nose, and her mouth were all exactly right for that face. So she was the girl in the other car Espie had seen through a blur.

The officer behind the desk said, "Juvenile is down this hall, right past that sign."

Espie watched Mrs. Summers and Allison walk away. Allison's tailored jeans and print shirt covered a perfect figure. Denise said something was bugging Allison, but Espie couldn't imagine how anybody who looked like that could have problems. She was the prettiest girl Espie had ever seen.

CHAPTER 4

Espie took off her coat. Sergeant Ernie Jackson asked, "Did you have a nice New Year's?" Espie told him briefly about the accident. "How long is Denise going to be in the hospital?" he asked.

"The doctor's not sure," Espie said, and hung up her coat.

The phone rang. Espie told Sergeant Jackson, "I'll get it," and pressed the flashing button. "Northeast Division, Explorer Sanchez speaking, may I help you, please?"

A woman said, "My old man just got ripped off."

The voice gave no indication of age. Espie asked, "Is this your husband or your father?"

"My father was a man. He'd never let kids take his money."

Espie held a pencil over a report sheet. "May I have your name, please?" she asked.

"Sheila Randall."

Espie wrote it in the block letters she had learned at the police academy. "How much money was taken?" she asked.

"Two hundred dollars. His whole week's salary."

Espie held back a whistle, not at the amount taken, but at the idea that somebody made two hundred bucks a week. "May I talk to your husband, please? I'll need descriptions."

The woman swore. "He won't give descriptions. He's scared. Scared of a bunch of kids."

Espie heard a man's voice. "They're Avenues. I'm not ratting on a gang."

The woman shouted, "Avenues! A bunch of kids."

Espie said, "Ma'am, if your husband doesn't want to talk, I . . ."

The woman said, "He'll talk when I get through with him." The phone slammed in Espie's ear.

She turned to Sergeant Jackson. "It's going to be one of those days."

A door opened down the hall and Mary Parks hurried toward Espie while Allison Summers and her mother moved to the outside door. Parks looked closely at Espie as though looking for signs of the crash. "I didn't know you'd been in an accident until I looked at the report. How's Denise?"

"She's in traction." Allison stopped and turned. "She's hurting pretty bad," Espie said, more to Allison than to Parks.

Mrs. Summers took a step toward Parks. The officer said, "This is Espie Sanchez. She was in the other car Monday night."

The woman came closer. "I'm sorry about your friend."

"Yeah, I'll tell her that."

"It wasn't my fault," Allison said.

"I'll tell her that, too," Espie said, her voice tight.

Mrs. Summers said, "The boy was drunk. Allison should never have gotten in the car with him."

Allison glanced at her mother and moved toward the

32

door. Parks walked with her. "Remember what I told you, Allison. Never ride with anybody who's been drinking. If you can't get a ride with anybody else, call your mother."

Mrs. Summers said, "I told her I'd go get her anyplace, anytime."

Mary Parks said. "And if a soft drink tastes funny, don't drink it. Some kids think slipping stuff in somebody's drink is a lot of fun, but you saw what happened." Parks opened the door and held it for Mrs. Summers and Allison. "Try not to let this bother you. It wasn't your fault."

"Thank you for being so nice," Allison said. She glanced at Espie and hurried out.

Parks went back to the desk. Espie asked, "If she was drunk Monday night, why didn't the police run her in?"

"She wasn't driving, and she doesn't have a record. It was better to release her to her parents and have her come in for counseling than run her through this place New Year's Eve."

The phone rang and Sergeant Jackson picked it up. "It's for you," he told Parks a moment later.

"I'll get it in my office," she said. She told Espie, "I'll give you a ride home at six. Okay?"

Espie nodded. She liked Parks's quick speech and walk. She was slightly built, but Espie figured Parks could change the whole world if she set her mind to it.

The phone rang, and Espie picked it up. "Northeast Division, Explorer Sanchez speaking, may I help you, please?"

The call was from a purse-snatch victim, and Espie took down the information that would be radioed to the police car closest to the scene. More calls came in. Espie handled them, and the people who walked into the station from the street. She filed reports. She even helped an arresting officer double-check crates of stolen property. When she had met Denise last May and learned Explorers didn't get money for working, Espie thought they were out of their skulls. But Espie liked working the desk, and she was usually sorry when it was time to go off duty. But this time, when Mary Parks came out of her office ready to leave, Espie grabbed her coat and hurried out with her so she could get home to ask Mrs. Garcia how Denise was.

"She want to come home," Mrs. Garcia said while she cooked hamburgers to serve with frijoles.

"Did any of the L.E.E.G.s go see her?"

"Rosemary and Sally. But they go before I get there." She put the hamburgers on a plate. "Denise wants you to ask her teachers for her books and her lessons tomorrow. She does not want to get behind in her studies."

Espie spooned frijoles on her dish. "I'll go see her teachers after school," she said, and ate while Mrs. Garcia told her about a girl she had met on the bus. "She say she look for work because her father is dead, and her mother is sick. I wish I can help her, but . . ." Mrs. Garcia didn't finish her sentence. Espie knew what she meant. Mrs. Garcia was always helping somebody. Her bureau was full of pictures of girls she had been foster mother to. And she was always wishing she had room for more than two girls at a time.

"You go rest. I'll wash the dishes," Espie said, and wished there were more Mrs. Garcia's to go around.

The next morning, Espie stalled around the house until Mrs. Garcia finally said, "Espie, if you do not go, you will be late for school."

"I'm leaving," she said, but she made one last trip to the bathroom. The head at Franklin Heights was always filthy, and she tried not to use it. There wasn't even any toilet paper. The teachers said it was because students

34

clogged up toilets with it, but everybody knew it was to keep kids from using the paper to roll joints.

When Espie came out of the bathroom, Mrs. Garcia gave her her lunch bag. "Thanks," Espie said and hurried down the steps. But when she was out of sight of the house, she slowed down.

She really hated to go to school after the two-week Christmas vacation. She thought about hitching a ride to Pasadena. The floats were still on display in Victory Park. The flowers would be wilted, but looking at floats would beat sitting through classes. She turned on Broadway. She had to go to school. She'd said she'd get Denise's books, and if she came home without them, Mrs. Garcia would know she'd ditched. Besides, she had to keep her C average to remain a L.E.E.G. 1975337

Espie headed for the gym. She didn't mind P.E., but she hated it first period because the teacher made the kids change to shorts no matter how cold it was. Espie took off her sweater and put on her short-sleeved blouse. She was shivering before she even got outside.

She went through the sit-ups and push-ups without even breathing hard. During the physical torture at the police academy she had found muscles she didn't know she had. It had been rough and, as her teacher sat on the bench in her sweatsuit while she counted jumping jacks, Espie wondered if the woman could make it through the Academy. Probably not. She was too flabby.

After the jumping jacks, they ran around the track. By the time the class finished, Espie was warm. But the shower set her shivering again. She got dressed quickly and headed for her biology class, glad the room was on the sunny side of the building.

When classes finished, Espie hurried to Denise's locker

to get her books. She just got the door open when she saw Allison Summers hurry toward her. A jabber of voices filled the hall. Kids pushed past them. Allison whispered, "That was the first time I was in a police station. You won't tell anybody about it, will you?"

"Explorers don't fink on people they see there," Espie said. She piled five of Denise's books on top of her own two.

"You on a study binge?"

"They belong to Denise. She asked me to bring them to her."

Allison said, "I'm really sorry about the accident."

"You've already said that." Espie pushed the locker shut with her elbow and faced Allison. "Look, Officer Parks said it wasn't your fault."

A guy bumped into Espie, and she dropped one of the books. Allison picked it up, and Espie reached for it. "I have to get moving if I'm going to catch Denise's teachers before they split."

Allison clutched the book. "It really *wasn't* my fault, you know."

The hall was almost empty now. Allison took a couple of books from Espie. "Let me help you carry those," she said. She looked scared to death of being left alone in the hall.

Espie stared at her, then shrugged. "Sure, come on," she said.

When Espie finished talking to Denise's teachers, Allison was still holding the books. "Let me give you a ride home," she said.

"Why?" Espie asked. Nobody ever offered her a ride home.

"Well, you have all those books, and my car's just down the street. Where do you live?"

36

"Right off Daly. It's up Broadway and . . ."

"I know where it is. I live on Mt. Washington."

"You do? Carlos and I were up there a few weeks ago helping the police look for a kid."

"Did you find him?"

"He was dead," Espie said, remembering the terrible coldness of the boy's lips when she tried to give him mouth-to-mouth resuscitation. Suddenly, she didn't want to be alone either. "Look, if you don't mind giving me a ride. These books *are* heavy."

Allison smiled for the first time since they met in the hall. "Want to stop for something to eat?" she asked, and started to walk toward her car.

"I'd better get right home," Espie said. There was no reason to say she never had money to stop for something to eat, especially to a girl who drove a new red Firebird.

"My folks gave it to me for Christmas," Allison said when she saw Espie staring at the car.

"How did they get it under the tree?" Espie said. Allison laughed, and they got in.

"Carlos your boyfriend?" Allison asked after she'd pulled out into the traffic.

Espie tensed when a car came out of a side street in front of them. "He's just a friend. His mother and Mrs. Garcia are in the altar society at Holy Trinity." Allison glanced at Espie. "Mrs. Garcia's my foster mother," Espie explained.

"Your folks dead?"

"Denise said you were new in school. You must be new in the neighborhood, too."

Allison stopped for a red light. "Why do you say that?"

"Kids don't ask questions like that around here. If people want to tell you their business, they'll tell you."

"I didn't mean to get personal. I just wondered. . . ."

The light turned green, and Allison pressed on the gas pedal. "We've only been here a month. My father has a law firm downtown, and he got tired of driving back and forth from the Valley. My mother doesn't like the area, but she likes the house on the hill. And she likes being just ten minutes from the Music Center. She's a stage nut. She goes to every play down there." Allison glanced at Espie. "You ever go to one?"

"I've never even seen the Music Center."

"But it's only a few minutes from here."

"Yeah, well Santa Claus was all out of cars and tickets to the Music Center when he got to my house this year," Espie said. She pointed to the corner. "Turn here. I'll tell you when to stop."

Allison asked, "What did I say wrong now?"

"I'm real sorry your mother has to pass through our area to get from her hill to wherever she's going."

"But . . ." Allison said.

"And you might as well learn the area is called the barrio, and it's the only place I know." Allison tried to interrupt her, but Espie kept talking. "I haven't been to the Music Center. Big deal. I haven't been lots of places. Until I joined the Explorers I hadn't been anyplace except when I was running away from home. Once I got to San Diego before the cops picked me up. The last time I got as far as York and Figueroa." Allison glanced at her. "That's right—a couple of miles from here. I figured the cops were getting smarter, or I was getting dumber." She pointed to her house. "It's the white one over there."

Allison stopped, and Espie began to pile the books in her arms. "And just so you'll get the whole scene—my folks aren't dead. My father took off when I was twelve, and my mother's a drunk who doesn't want me. How does that grab you?" Espie opened the door.

Allison said, "Don't go."

"Why? You want to tell me about your rich grand-mother?"

"It's not like that at all. I was just talking."

"Well, I don't like the way you talk." Espie struggled out with the books and hurried up the walk. A couple fell before she reached the porch. She kept walking and put the others on the steps. When she turned around, Allison was holding the books in a trembling hand.

"Don't leave me alone. Please," she said.

Espie wanted to tell her to get back in her Firebird and get the hell up her hill, but she was too curious about what was bugging Allison.

"Come on in," she said and unlocked the door.

CHAPTER 5

When Espie entered the house, the familiar odor of chiles and beans that clung to the old walls and furniture greeted her. Espie liked it. What she didn't like was the silence of an empty house. Mrs. Garcia was always there to ask, "You have a nice day at school?" But today as Allison closed the door behind her they were alone, and Espie missed the familiar question.

"Mrs. Garcia's at the hospital," she told Allison.

"What's it like . . . ?" Allison didn't finish the question.

"What's what like?"

"Never mind. It was one of those personal questions."

"Sit down," Espie said, and pointed to the couch. Allison sat on the cushion that had the broken spring and moved over to the next one. Espie told her, "I'll make a deal. You answer my personal question and I'll answer yours."

"What do you want to know?" Allison asked warily.

Espie sat opposite her and swung her leg over the worn arm of the chair. "Why are you so afraid to be alone?"

Allison gave a short laugh. "I'm not afraid to be alone."

"Come off it. You've latched on to me like a habit."

"Maybe I just like you."

"Nobody gets that crazy about me."

Allison fingered the catch on her purse and kept her eyes down. "I guess the accident is finally getting to me. You know, Alex getting killed. I didn't really know him or anything. I'd only met him a couple of hours before the accident. He said he'd give me a ride home after the guy I went to the party with took off with another girl. We hardly even talked to each other. But he's dead, and I don't like to think about it."

Espie rolled her hair around her finger and waited for Allison to go on. "Besides, if I'm alone I'll need . . ." A car stopped outside. Allison asked, "That Mrs. Garcia?"

"Mrs. Garcia rides the bus."

"Want to go pick her up?"

Espie swung her leg to the floor. "Great, then we can see Denise." She sat back. "It won't work. Mrs. Garcia's probably on her way back, and we'd miss her."

"Then let's go get her at the bus stop so she won't have to walk home."

Espie stood up. "She should be there pretty soon."

When they were back in the car, Allison asked, "What's it like living with a foster mother?" She smiled at Espie. "That's *my* personal question."

Espie shrugged. "It beats living with my mother and her boyfriends."

"Does she live far from here?"

"A couple of miles."

"Ever see her?"

"Not if I can help it." Allison glanced at Espie. "Don't people say things like that in the Valley?" Espie asked.

Allison didn't answer. Instead she said, "You still didn't tell me what it's like living with a foster mother."

Espie said, "Park along here. She'll be getting off at that

corner." Allison slowed down, and Espie said, "I guess it's like living with your real mother. If you get a good one, you've got it made. If you get a drunk like my mother, it's a bummer." Allison hit the curb when she stopped. Espie said, "Hey, your mother's not a boozer, is she?"

Allison turned off the engine. Espie noticed her lips tremble. "Not unless a cocktail before dinner makes her a boozer."

"Cocktails? My mother swigs it out of the bottle." A bus pulled up and stopped. Espie watched the people get off. "She's not on that one," she said.

People glanced in the car as they passed. Espie said, "When the cops picked me up that last time, I'd have landed in juvey if I hadn't gone to Mrs. Garcia's. I figured I could run away from her place anytime I wanted."

"Why haven't you?"

Espie shrugged. "I've got a lot going for me there— food, a place to sleep. And Mrs. Garcia's okay. She doesn't bug me much." Another bus stopped. Mrs. Garcia wasn't on that one, either. "But she won't let me go out except to Explorer meetings and things."

"Why not?"

"She's afraid of the gangs. And I guess she's still living in the old days. You know, girls didn't go anyplace except with their family until some guy came along and married them." Espie chuckled. "Then they didn't go anyplace."

Allison said, "Think she'd let you join the youth band at church?"

"You mean the kids who sing at nine-thirty Mass?"

Allison nodded. "I joined a couple of weeks ago because I didn't know anybody around here. They practice every Tuesday night. Except they're holding a special rehearsal tomorrow for Epiphany this Sunday."

"I don't play anything," Espie said.

"I can't play anything either. I just sing background."

"I used to sing a lot with my father," Espie said. A couple of guys passed by and said something in Spanish.

"What did they say?" Allison asked.

"They said they could get five bucks apiece for the hubcaps."

Allison looked in the rearview mirror. "They're moving away," she said. She leaned against the door. "Think Mrs. Garcia would let you join the Celebration Group?"

"I don't know. She's pretty hung-up about going to eight o'clock Mass."

"Can't you go to nine-thirty Mass without her?"

"No way. She wants us all to go together," Espie said. But she liked the idea of getting out of the house every Tuesday. "How would I get to rehearsals?"

"I could pick you up."

"Maybe they wouldn't let me in."

Allison laughed. "If you can hum, you're in."

A bus pulled up, and Espie said, "There she is. Listen, don't say anything about the group. I'll ask her when we're alone." She opened the door and got out.

Mrs. Garcia stared at her, then at the car. "Espie, what you do here?"

"Allison gave me a ride from school, and we decided to pick you up so you wouldn't have to walk home."

Mrs. Garcia smiled. "That is nice," she said as Espie hopped in the back. Mrs. Garcia eased into the front seat, and Espie said, "Mrs. Garcia, this is Allison Summers."

Mrs. Garcia got the door half closed before she stopped and turned. "You are the girl who was in the accident with Denise and Espie?"

Espie saw Allison's hands begin to shake, and she gripped the steering wheel to steady them. "I'm sorry about that," she said.

"It is a terrible thing, but it is not your fault," Mrs. Garcia said, and closed the door.

Allison started the car, and Espie said, "How's Denise?"

"She say the pain is still bad, and she want to come home. And . . . And it will be a long time." Allison pulled away from the curb, and Mrs. Garcia said, "It is a beautiful car."

"My folks gave it to me for Christmas."

"They are rich," Mrs. Garcia said.

"They're not rich. My father's just a lawyer. . . ."

"I got Denise's books," Espie interrupted so she wouldn't have to listen to Allison's story again. Besides, what wasn't rich to Allison was plenty rich to Mrs. Garcia.

Allison stopped in front of the house, and Mrs. Garcia said, "You come eat with us?"

"I'd better get home. My mother should be there now."

Mrs. Garcia got out, and Espie followed. Allison said, "Want a ride to school tomorrow?"

"Sure."

"I'll pick you up at seven thirty, okay?"

"Okay," Espie said, and closed the door. Allison switched on the headlights and pulled away.

Mrs. Garcia said, "She is a nice girl."

Espie smiled. If Mrs. Garcia liked Allison, Espie was one step closer to getting out on Tuesday nights.

While they ate tortillas and warmed-over chile, Mrs. Garcia told Espie about Denise. "She say she has pain in her right leg, but she no feel pain when the doctor sticks pins in her feet."

"Why is he sticking pins in her feet?"

Mrs. Garcia shrugged. "She say that what he do, but she no feel it. Before I leave, I ask the nurse why Denise no feel the pins. She say if Denise does not feel them soon, they will operate to see what is wrong."

"Her spine's busted, that's what's wrong," Espie said, and wondered if anybody in that hospital knew what they were doing.

"They know her spine is hurt."

"I wouldn't bet on it," Espie said.

Mrs. Garcia buttered a tortilla. "How you know Allison?" she asked.

Espie told her about meeting Allison at the lockers and how she offered to give Espie a ride home because she had so many books to carry.

"She is a nice girl," Mrs. Garcia said again, and Espie figured it was time to tell her about the singing group.

Mrs. Garcia said she knew about the group. She had even heard them the few times she had gone to nine-thirty Mass. And she liked the idea of Espie "singing to God and His Mother," but she didn't like the idea of weekly practice.

"You have Explorer meetings Thursdays. If you practice singing every Tuesday, you will not have time to study for school, and you must keep a C average."

"I'll study after school on Tuesdays instead of after supper." Espie began to clear the table. "I can keep a C."

Mrs. Garcia went to the sink and started to run the water for the dishes. "I do not know. But . . ." Espie waited. Mrs. Garcia finished filling the dish pan. Finally she smiled. "I think it will make God happy if you do this, and I will go to nine-thirty Mass to hear you," she said.

"Hey, that's great. I'll tell Allison tomorrow," Espie said, and carried the rest of the dishes to the sink.

Allison didn't come at seven thirty, and Espie had just decided to start walking when she saw the Firebird. "Sorry I'm late, but I have trouble getting going in the morning," Allison said when Espie got in the car.

"I'm not in a hurry to get to school, but I was hoping

you'd get here so Mrs. Garcia wouldn't change her mind about letting me go to rehearsal tonight."

"You can go? That's great." They stopped for a kid in the crosswalk. "What did she say about going to nine-thirty Mass?"

"She's going to come hear me."

The car moved again. "Maybe Denise will join the group when she gets out of the hospital."

"She might not be able to walk when she gets out." The words slipped out before Espie could stop herself.

A car stopped for a red light, and Allison almost rammed into it. "Why not?"

"There's something wrong with her spine."

"You didn't tell me that yesterday."

"I didn't want to talk about it yesterday. And I don't want to talk about it now."

The light changed and traffic moved again. "When will you know if she'll be able to walk?"

"Maybe next week. They're talking about an operation."

Allison didn't say anything the rest of the way. And when she got out of the car, Espie said, "Want me to meet you here at three?"

"Yeah, sure," Allison said, and Espie started for the gym. Before she reached the door she saw Allison get back in the car and drive away. A couple of kids stepped off the curb into the crosswalk. Allison didn't slow down, and they jumped back on the curb to safety.

The car wasn't there when school finished, and Espie walked home wondering if Allison was sick. The phone was ringing when she put her key in the lock. She opened the door and ran. "Where's Manny?" a man asked when she picked up the phone.

"You got the wrong number," Espie said.

She waited for Allison to call. When the phone hadn't rung by four, Espie got the phone book and looked up the name *Summers*. There were dozens of people listed under that name. She didn't remember hearing Allison say her father's name. And Espie didn't know what street the Summers lived on. She closed the book and stared at the phone.

Why didn't she call? She knew how much Espie wanted to go to the rehearsal. She was glad Mrs. Garcia wasn't home to ask, "What time Allison come for you?" Espie opened the phone book again. She had to have an answer to that question before Mrs. Garcia came home.

She ran her finger down the names and saw *Ellery Summers, atty.* His office was on Spring Street and his home number started with a 7 instead of a 2, the way her phone number did. That's probably their old number, Espie thought, and dialed information. Within minutes she had a local number for Ellery Summers. She dialed and willed somebody to pick up the phone, but nobody did. She was going to hang up when a girl answered. Her voice was soft and sleepy.

"Allison?"

"Yes."

"This is Espie. What happened to you this morning?"

Silence. Then Allison said, "I didn't feel well."

"What's the matter with you?"

"I'm okay now."

She didn't sound okay, but Espie said, "Can you go to rehearsal tonight?"

"What rehearsal?"

"The rehearsal at church. You sure you're okay?"

"Sure, I'm fine. I'll be there at six," Allison said, and hung up before Espie could say anything else.

When Mrs. Garcia came home, Espie asked how Denise

was. "She say the pain does not stop. I see the doctor. He say he think he will operate."

"Does Denise know?"

Mrs. Garcia shook her head. "The doctor no tell her. He say it is better for now so she will not worry."

Mrs. Garcia put on her apron. "She is happy to get her books. The nurse put up the bed a little, and Denise say she read when I leave. She say she is glad tomorrow is Saturday so she can see you."

Espie began to set the table. "Did you tell her about the singing group?"

"I tell her. She say she like to join." Mrs. Garcia took eggs out of the refrigerator. "We have scrambled eggs and frijoles," she said, and cracked the eggs.

After supper Espie took a shower and put on a clean pair of jeans and her orange top. She brushed her hair, then put on lipstick and eye make-up. Maybe there'd be some nice-looking guys.

Allison came at six fifteen. "Hi, how you feeling?" Espie said.

"I'm okay. I just felt a little sick this morning." Allison offered Espie a mint and moved away from the curb.

"Did Mrs. Garcia go see Denise today?"

Espie nodded. "Denise is still hurting pretty bad."

"They still talking about an operation?"

"Yeah. It scares me to think about it.

When Allison stopped the car in front of the church, she picked up her purse and fingered the catch. "I have to go to the bathroom. I'll meet you inside." She hurried to the side of the church.

Espie ran after her. She opened the door to the head. "You feeling sick again?" she asked before she saw the bottle of whiskey in Allison's hand.

"I drink—a little," Allison said, and Espie walked away.

CHAPTER 6

Espie hurried around the corner of the church and bumped into a guy carrying a couple of drums.

He gave them to her. "You're just in time to help me carry these in."

Espie shoved them back at him. "Carry your own drums," she said. She heard somebody laugh. She turned around. "What are you laughing at?" she asked the guy holding a guitar case. There was still no sign of Allison.

The guy nodded toward the drummer. "Joaquin finally met somebody he couldn't unload the drums on."

Espie walked away. The guy ran in front of her. "Don't go," he said.

"Why? You want me to carry your guitar?"

He smiled. "My name's Rick Fernando. You joining the group?"

"I was going to, but . . ."

Allison came around the corner, and Joaquin said, "Hey, Allison, take these, will you?"

"Sure," Allison said. She turned to Espie. "Did Rick tell you he runs the group?"

Rick laughed. "The group runs me."

Espie liked the way he looked at her when he laughed. He seemed to be saying, "Stick around. We'll have fun." He put his hand on her arm and guided her toward the door of the hall on the side of the church. "Come on meet the others," he said.

Allison passed them with the two small drums. "Come on, Espie. You'll have a good time in spite of them."

Espie turned to leave, but Rick was behind her and Joaquin was behind him with the bass drum. Someone from inside the room said, "Hi, Allison."

Another voice asked, "Hey, Rick, who's the new chick?"

Rick said, "Espie . . ." He asked her, "What's your last name?"

"Sanchez."

Espie had been eased into the room by Rick and Joaquin, and everybody was asking her what school she went to. They seemed glad she came, and Espie liked that. Allison had put down the drums at the other end of the room and was laughing at something Joaquin said.

A couple more kids came in, and somebody said, "Hey, Georgie, where'd you get that crazy shirt?"

"I made it," Georgie said. He pulled his knit cap lower on his head and glared.

Espie had seen that action on the street. It meant a fight for anybody who laughed. Allison giggled, and Espie's eyes went from her to Georgie. He started for Allison, and Espie stepped in front of him. "I think it's a great shirt," she told him. Everybody stood frozen around her.

Georgie leaned toward her. "Where'd you come from?"

"Joaquin's bass drum," Espie said.

Georgie's body loosened, and he chuckled. Rick said, "Okay, gang, let's get on it," and people moved toward the mikes. He whispered to Espie, "Nice job." Aloud he said, "The first song Sunday will be 'We Three Kings.' "

Joaquin said, "We don't have to practice that. We've been practicing it since Christmas."

Rick said, "And you're still not together."

Joaquin said, "I'd like to try some togetherness with Allison."

Everybody laughed, and Rick said, "Espie, you alto or soprano?"

Espie shrugged. "I just sing. But I don't know that song."

Rick handed her a sheet of paper. "Here're the words. Listen a few minutes. When you think you can follow, join in." There were four mikes with two or three people at each one. "Come on, you can use my mike," he said.

Espie stood beside him, and he lowered the mike for her. Everybody was talking, and he shouted, "Hey, hold it down, you guys." The voices died away. He tapped his foot. On the third beat, he signaled with a nod of his head, and he and the other guitarist started the introduction to the song. Joaquin tapped his drums softly. The kids sang, " 'We three kings of Orient are, bearing gifts we traverse afar.' " Espie recognized the Christmas carol and joined in the refrain. " 'O, star of wonder, star of night,' " she sang softly, and stopped singing at the end of the chorus. The others went on, " 'Born a babe on Bethlehem's . . .' "

Rick said, "Hold it." Everybody stopped and looked at him. "I heard three different 'borns.' "

Georgie said, "So we'll get three babes."

Rick said, "I want only one babe and one 'born.' Let's do it again from the top."

They started over, and Espie sang the chorus a little louder this time. Rick smiled at her and she smiled back.

They did the song three more times, and somebody

always came in late on the chorus. Rick said, "We can't use up any more time on this one. We'll have to go to the next song."

Georgie said, "We got three kings so what's wrong with three babes?"

The kids laughed, and Rick shouted, "Okay, let's do 'Turn, Turn, Turn.' " He said to Espie, "You know this one, don't you?" She nodded. "Okay, then sing out. This is the Celebration Group. We're supposed to let people know how happy we are." He gave the signal and the music started.

Espie sang with the others, " 'To every thing, turn, turn, turn. There is a season, turn, turn, turn. . . .' " A few kids danced in place while they sang. " 'A time of love, a time of hate.' " Rick did a crazy dance step and winked at Espie.

The group was good. And they looked like they were having a great time. Even Georgie was smiling.

When they finished, Espie said to Rick, "You don't do that dance in church, do you?" She figured Mrs. Garcia would yank her out of the group if he did.

Rick shook his head. "I don't think God would care if I did, but a lot of little old ladies would go running to Father Acosta, and he'd hassle us."

Allison said, "Can't we take a break?"

Rick looked at his watch. "Okay, ten minutes, then we'll practice the new version of the Our Father."

Espie saw Allison take off for the head. The others sat on the floor. Georgie asked, "Anybody wanna pitch pennies?" Nobody answered, and he tossed a coin.

Rick told Espie, "I'm glad Allison brought you." His smile came easy. His black hair hung an inch from the collar of his embroidered shirt.

"She says you practice every Tuesday night."

"Did she tell you the rules?"

"She just said if I could hum I was in."

"We're tougher than that. I put new members near me so I can audition them without their knowing it. If they can't cut it, I tell them."

Espie put her thumbs in the belt loops of her jeans. "That what you're trying to tell me?"

"No, you made it." He grinned. "Besides, I'd bend the rules for you."

"Thanks—I think," Espie said.

"Can I give you a ride home?"

Espie wanted to say yes, but if she came home with Rick, Mrs. Garcia wouldn't let her join the group.

"I've got a ride."

"Allison won't care if you ride with me."

Allison had just opened the door. "Did I hear my name?" she asked. She had another mint in her mouth.

Rick said, "I'm going to give Espie a ride home, okay?"

Allison said, "It's okay with me." She looked at Espie. "But I thought you had a couple of things to do on the way home."

It took a moment for Espie to realize Allison had figured Mrs. Garcia wouldn't want Espie to come home with a guy. She said, "That's right. Maybe some other time, Rick."

One of the girls said, "Let's get back to work. There's a program I want to watch at nine o'clock."

Rick reached for his guitar. "Okay, maybe next time," he told Espie.

"Yeah," she said, and took her place beside him.

He told the group. "I wrote this music for the Our Father because I wanted to speed it up. But Sunday you were so slow, I felt like I was pulling everybody up a mountain." He told Espie, "Just listen to the music. You'll pick it up, okay?" Espie nodded, and he gave the signal to begin.

" 'Our Father, Who art in heaven, hallowed be Thy name,' " Rick said, "Faster," and, without missing a note, the kids picked up the pace. " 'Thy kingdom come, Thy will be done.' "

As Espie listened she watched the others. Joaquin was at the drums. Allison and two girls were singing at one mike. Georgie was holding the music sheet for a guy named Ozzie who was playing a guitar, and two guys were singing harmony at another mike.

Ozzie said, "Georgie's shaking the music sheet so much I can't see the notes."

"Hey, man, my hands are still as the wind."

Ozzie said, "Yeah, and we're having a hurricane."

Everybody cracked up, and Rick said, "Okay, one more time from the top."

Espie watched Allison. She didn't look like she'd been drinking. But there were all kinds of boozers. Some looked drunk after a few drinks. Some didn't show it until they'd downed a pint or more.

" 'For Thine is the Kingdom and the Power and the Glory, forever,' " the group sang, and Rick said, "Okay now, a slow Amen."

When they finished, they went over the parts of the song Rick wanted to move faster, then they sang, "Go Tell It on the Mountain." Espie knew the song and joined in. Rick winked and did his crazy dance step again, and Espie wished she could ride home with him.

They quit at eight thirty, and there was a lot of horsing around while Joaquin tried to get people to help him with his drums again. He did such a good con job, he strolled out carrying only the cymbals.

54

Rick walked with Espie and Allison to the car. "See you Sunday at nine fifteen," he told Espie.

"I'll be there," Espie said. He shut the door, and Espie locked it. Allison waved and pulled away from the curb.

"You really wanted to go home with him, didn't you?" Allison asked. Espie nodded. "I'm sorry I messed you up. I have to talk to you. That's why I said you had things to do on the way home."

"I thought you said that because you knew Mrs. Garcia wouldn't let me join the group if I came home with him."

"I didn't know that."

Espie swung her body around and faced Allison. "And I didn't know you drink."

"That's what I want to talk to you about. I haven't had a drink since New Year's Eve—until today."

"Three days. Is that a record for you or something?"

Allison shook her head. "I stayed off the stuff for a week when I started at Franklin Heights. You know, I thought new neighborhood, new life. But I couldn't handle a new school without booze. But after the accident I told myself I'd never take another drink. It's been hell. That's why I didn't want to be alone Thursday. I knew if I was, I'd get a bottle. I was doing okay until you told me Denise might not walk again."

"Your drinking is what made her that way."

"I wasn't driving that car."

They reached Mrs. Garcia's house, but Allison drove by it. "Hey, you missed the house."

She stopped a block away. "I have to talk to you."

"You've been talking to me, and you haven't said anything I want to hear." Espie glanced out the back window. "Take me back. It's not smart to park in this neighborhood."

"The doors are locked."

"Ever hear of guns?"

Allison started the car. "Then we'll drive around until I'm finished talking."

"You finished talking to me when I saw that bottle in your hand."

"Haven't you ever had a drink?"

"Sure, but I never killed a guy or crippled anybody."

"I wasn't driving that car," Allison said again. Her voice begged Espie to understand.

"What do you want me to do? You want me to tell you it's all right to drink? Okay, it's all right to drink. Now take me home."

"Damn it. I'm asking for help."

"Why me?"

"Because I don't have anybody else."

"How about your folks?"

"They don't think I've got a problem."

"Why not?"

"Most of their friends let their kids have liquor at parties."

"Having booze at parties and carrying a bottle in your purse isn't exactly the same thing."

"They don't know about that."

"Why don't you tell them?"

Allison stopped the car in the middle of the deserted street and looked at Espie. "They don't really care. My father's hardly ever home. He doesn't have to drive back and forth to the Valley so he stays longer at the office. And my mother's always at some play or meeting or something. I've given up trying to talk to them."

"Keep moving," Espie said, and the car rolled again. "How long have you been drinking?"

"Four years. Since I was twelve."

"Why do you do it?"

"It helps me feel good when there's nobody around. And when there's people, it helps me not be afraid to talk to them."

They were cruising through almost-empty streets. Occasionally a dog barked at them while he ran beside the car or the headlights picked up the flash of a cat's eyes. The barrio had been left to the animals until daylight.

Espie asked, "Why did you start?"

"My mother made me go to a lot of parties, and I was so ugly nobody ever danced with me. And when I tried to talk to people, I stuttered. So I just got more and more afraid of going to parties." Espie couldn't imagine Allison ever being ugly, but it was easy to feel that way when everybody's having a good time, and you're all alone. She softened a little.

"So, how did you begin to drink?"

"One night before a party I found a pitcher of unfinished martinis on the bar. My mother always had a couple of drinks before a party—to turn on the personality, she always told my father—so I poured the martini stuff in a glass and took a sip. It tasted terrible. I started to pour it back in the pitcher, then I thought about the party I was going to. I finished off two drinks, and by the time my mother dropped me off at the party, I felt great. I went in smiling and started to talk to a guy about something. I don't remember what, but it didn't matter. He asked me to dance, and I stayed on the floor all night."

"Why should I help you?"

"You know about booze. Your mother's a drunk."

"My mother didn't start drinking until five years ago." Espie was surprised at the anger in her voice. "And she wasn't driving a Firebird at sixteen. She was a waitress supporting four brothers." Allison turned another corner. "You going to drive us around all night?"

Allison said, "Please help me." The words sounded like a whimper. She glanced at Espie, then back at the road. "Okay, I wasn't driving the car New Year's Eve, but that accident was my fault. The guy I went to the party with took off with another girl because I wouldn't stop drinking, so Alex said he'd take me home after he'd had some coffee and something to eat. I was so mad at being dumped, I told him he'd take me right then or forget it. That's why he hit you. He was so drunk, he didn't even see the car."

"You told the cops you hadn't been drinking."

"I'll take you home," Allison said. She sounded scared. And alone. Espie knew what it was like to be both.

"I don't know how to help you."

"Ride with me to school so I'll get there. Come with me to the Celebration Group rehearsals so I won't quit it. Let me call you when I'm alone. Please be my friend."

Espie thought about Rick. She couldn't get to rehearsals without Allison. "Sure I'll be your friend," she said.

CHAPTER 7

Before she got out of the Firebird, Espie asked for the half-empty whiskey bottle. Allison gave it up reluctantly, and Espie put it under her shirt in the waistband of her jeans so she could get it in the house to throw away.

As soon as she opened the door she heard the foot-pedal sewing machine. Mrs. Garcia looked up when Espie reached the kitchen. "You have a nice time?"

Espie nodded. "It was fun."

"They are nice girls and boys?"

"Yeah, they're really nice," Espie said, feeling the bulge of the bottle at her waist.

"What you do?"

Espie told her the names of the songs they sang and how she had done more listening than singing. "But the guy who leads the group said I'll pick it up."

"You like singing to God?"

"Yeah, I like it. I really do," Espie said, and Mrs. Garcia looked so pleased as she went back to her sewing, Espie didn't tell her how fast the kids sang the Our Father and how nice Rick was.

She put the bottle in her dresser drawer, then took it out again. Mrs. Garcia would see it when she put clothes in. Espie knew she should have just emptied the stuff and left the bottle in the gutter, but she didn't have the guts to dump whiskey in front of Allison.

She went to the closet and placed it on the shelf, but she was too short to put it far enough to hide it. Finally, she shoved it under her mattress, then sneaked it out to the trash can the next morning while Mrs. Garcia was getting dressed to go to the hospital.

When they got there, Espie hurried up the hill that led to the entrance but slowed down when she got too far ahead of Mrs. Garcia. Espie was surprised at how anxious she was to see Denise.

A doctor stopped them when they reached the orthopedic ward. "Mrs. Garcia, I was hoping I'd still be here when you came."

"Dr. Wallace, how is Denise?"

"She's responding to strong stimuli and . . ."

Espie interrupted him. "You'll have to explain that to Mrs. Garcia."

The doctor grinned. Espie wondered if he knew she was the one who needed the explanation. "It means she can feel a pinprick if we press hard enough."

Mrs. Garcia asked, "That is good?"

"We might not have to do surgery." Espie felt her body relax. The doctor said, "When the tests we did the night of the accident showed damage to the spinal cord, we hoped traction would take care of it. But when Denise didn't respond to our stimuli . . ." He smiled at Espie, then turned back to Mrs. Garcia to explain. "When Denise said she couldn't feel anything when we pricked her feet or applied hot and cold objects to them, we thought surgery was needed to repair the damage to the spine. But during my rounds this morning, she said she thought she felt something."

Espie said, "How can she think she felt something? You feel or you don't feel."

"It's not that way when the spine isn't sending signals to the brain. We haven't ruled out surgery, but the results this morning were encouraging. We'll see what happens tomorrow." He glanced at his watch. "I have to go."

Mrs. Garcia clutched his hand. "*Gracias,*" she said several times while she pumped it up and down.

"Don't say anything about this to Denise. I'll tell her if we have to do surgery," he said and walked to the elevator.

The head of Denise's bed was up, and she was reading when they came in. The bruises on her face were more purple and green than black and blue the way they'd been New Year's Day. She was still in the traction belt, and she looked like she'd lost weight.

"Did many of the L.E.E.G.s come?" Espie said after they greeted each other.

"Rosemary and Sally came. And Officer Parks. She brought the flowers." Denise nodded toward the pink and white carnations on the stand near the bed. "Carlos sent that card. And Roxanne and Alice came last night."

"Did Alice wear her gold bars?" Espie asked.

Denise laughed. "She gets carried away as Post captain. So what? I'll be hard-nosed too when I make captain." Denise looked down at her legs. "If I ever get out of here."

"You'll get out," Espie encouraged her.

"We went through this conversation when you were here New Year's Day," Denise said. She learned forward. "Is the youth group fun?"

"It's fun, but I don't know all the songs. Rick said I'd pick them up."

"Who's Rick?"

"He's the group's leader."

"How are the kids?" Denise asked.

"They're nice. You'll like them."

"What about Allison? I mean, she hardly talks to anybody at school, and Mrs. Garcia said you're so friendly with her, she even came to pick you up yesterday."

Mrs. Garcia said, "In her nice car. I think she is rich."

Espie said, "She's not rich. Her folks just have more money than we do."

Denise asked, "How did you get so friendly with her?"

"I just turned on my great charm, and she begged me to ride in the car with her."

Mrs. Garcia said, "I go to the bathroom. I will be back."

Espie sat down, and Denise said, "Hey, what's going on with this Rick?"

"Nothing's going on. He's just nice."

"You looked different when you said his name."

"You've been working with the cops too long. You're imagining things."

"Come on, level with me. You're only out of my sight a few days and you're Allison Summers's best friend, and you get this great romance going with some guy named Rick."

"Some romance. I saw the guy for two hours last night."

"What does he look like?"

"He's about five seven, black hair, black eyes. He plays the guitar for the group."

"Did you tell Mrs. Garcia about him?"

"You crazy? She'd never let me go to another rehearsal. You know how she feels about guys. She thinks we should be nuns or something."

"Yeah, well maybe it'll be different with Rick. He's got something going for him."

"What?"

"He's in a church group. Make it work for you."

Espie smiled. "Hey, I've got an idea." She stood up and began to pace. "When Mrs. Garcia gets back, you ask me about the songs we sang last night, and I'll tell you how hard they are to sing. Then I can say I wish Rick would come to the house and help me learn them. You know. Not can he come or anything like that. I can just say maybe I won't be able to keep up with the group because there's so many songs to learn, and it sure would be nice if Rick would help me."

"And make it sound like it would be a real hassle," Denise said. "Like he has a hundred other things he'd rather do, and you don't know if he'd even come. But the group is so important to him that he might."

"Think she'll go for it?"

"It can't hurt to try."

When Mrs. Garcia came back, she asked Denise, "How are your studies?"

"I'll be finished with the assignments Espie got for me by tomorrow."

"That is good. She can take them to school Monday and get more. You no want to get behind."

"I won't," Denise said, and looked at Espie. "What kind of songs do you sing with the group?"

After that, Espie and Denise kept the conversation going about how hard the songs were until Mrs. Garcia said, "Allison can teach you."

Espie said, "She can teach me the words but it's hard to sing without music."

Denise said, "Maybe you could get the guy who runs the group to help you. Doesn't he play an instrument?"

Denise was doing a great job. Espie said, "Yeah, he plays the guitar, but I don't know if he'd do it."

"You could ask him," Denise said.

"He's probably too busy," Espie said. And she and Denise talked about it while Mrs. Garcia listened. Finally, she said, "I think if you ask him he will do it."

Espie looked at her. "You really think so?"

"If he wants the group to sing good, he will do it."

Espie said, "I'll ask him at church tomorrow."

Mrs. Garcia said, "I think it is a good idea."

Espie was afraid if she looked at Denise, they would give the whole thing away. She picked up a get-well card on the table and looked at it. "How's the food in this place?" she asked finally.

"It's not bad, but I could sure go for a couple of Mrs. Garcia's tacos," Denise said, and they spent the rest of the time talking about the hospital, the doctors, and the nurses. And Denise complained about all of them. "They can't even tell me when I'll get out of here," she said.

Mrs. Garcia told her, "Maybe they do not know."

"They can't even tell me when I'm going to get out of traction. I don't think anybody knows anything."

"Maybe they know in a few days."

"That's what the doctors keep telling me," Denise said.

"See, I am smart like the doctors," Mrs. Garcia said. She looked so pleased with her little joke, Espie laughed, and so did Denise.

But she wasn't laughing when visiting hours ended. She looked like she was fighting back tears, and Mrs. Garcia said, "We will come right after Mass." She hugged Denise, who clung to her a long time before she let go.

"Good luck with the group tomorrow," she told Espie.

"Thanks. I'll tell you all about it, okay?" Espie said. When she got to the door she turned and waved. Denise was reaching for a Kleenex.

Carlos called at eight thirty to ask how Denise was

doing. "The doctor said she responded to strong stimuli this morning."

Carlos asked, "What the hell does that mean?"

"It means she can feel a pin go in her foot if he stabs her hard enough."

"Come on, Espie. What did he say?"

"He said maybe traction is taking care of the spinal injury, and they won't have to operate."

"That's what he said before."

"But this time I think even *he* believes it."

"That's terrific."

"Mrs. Garcia said her prayers have been answered, but I'll believe the great miracle when I see Denise walk out of that hospital."

Espie sat on the floor, her back against the wall, while they talked about the Explorers, and she told Carlos about the Celebration Group and about Rick. It was nine thirty when she hung up. The phone rang almost immediately.

Espie picked it up, and Allison said, "Where have you been?" Her words were slow and slurred.

"If you want me to help you quit drinking, you'll have to at least try to lay off the stuff," Espie said angrily.

"Some help you are. You weren't even home when I called today."

"I went to the hospital. The doctor says Denise may not need an operation," Espie said. She figured that might keep Allison off the sauce.

"She going to be able to walk?"

"She'll be joining the Celebration Group in no time." Allison didn't say anything. Espie said, "What's the matter? The news should make you feel better."

"Alex is dead," Allison whispered. The words covered Espie with a chill. "I need another drink," Allison told her.

"Look, if you drink now you may not make it to nine-thirty Mass. Then you won't see Joaquin."

"Do you think he likes me?"

"He sure acted that way last night."

"Why would he like me?"

"Because you're pretty, and you've got a great body." Espie searched for something else to say. "And you're fun to be with," she said a little too quickly because she didn't really think Allison was very good company.

"Only when I've had a few drinks. Any other time I can't even talk to people without shaking."

"I don't think you have trouble talking to people. I think you tell yourself that so you'll have an excuse to drink."

"That's not true. People scare me so much, I stutter."

"You didn't stutter when you met Mrs. Garcia."

"You don't believe anything I tell you," Allison said angrily.

Espie decided to back away. "Does Joaquin go to Franklin Heights?"

"He and Rick go to some school for boys. St. Damien, I think he said. Do you really think he likes me?" Allison asked again.

"He sure acts like he does."

"Guys don't like me for long."

Espie was getting tired of the conversation. When Mrs. Garcia called from the kitchen, "You go to bed now?" Espie was glad for the excuse to hang up.

She undressed and got into bed still angry at Allison. She had it all—parents, money, looks, a car—and still she drank. A lot of kids drank at Franklin Heights. But Espie figured they might have reasons to drink. Allison didn't. Espie huddled under the blankets. She'd had booze at parties. But she didn't have to drink. Why was it so hard for Allison to give it up?

CHAPTER 8

It was eight thirty, an hour before Mass, and Espie was nervous. She'd never sung for an audience. People at Mass weren't an audience, exactly, but they'd be there to hear her. Well, she didn't have to sing. She could mouth the words. But Rick would know she wasn't singing. She couldn't stay in the group if she didn't sing. She wondered what he'd say when she asked him to come to the house. Maybe he wouldn't come. She had figured he liked her because of the way he looked at her. But maybe he looked at all the girls that way.

She zipped up the blue dress Mrs. Garcia had made for her when Espie came to live with her. She hated dresses, but she liked the way this one made her look. He'd come. He had to come. As she examined herself in the mirror, she was glad she had the dress. Rick would like it.

She put on lipstick and a little eye make-up before she went to the living room to wait for Mrs. Garcia. "I will be ready soon. We do not want to be late for the singing," Mrs. Garcia said from the bedroom.

When she came out she wore a sweater over her black church dress and carried her rosary and the donation envelope. Espie figured Mrs. Garcia needed the money more than the church did, but every Sunday she put fifty cents in the envelope and gave Espie and Denise each a quarter to drop in the basket.

"You wear your coat?" Mrs. Garcia asked.

"I don't need it. It's warm enough," Espie said. She liked the coat, but she didn't want to hide the dress. She opened the front door and felt the warm sun on her face.

"Then you need your sweater."

"The sun's hot enough. I'll be okay," she said, and started out before Mrs. Garcia made her go back for the navy-blue sweater.

Several people coming from the eight o'clock Mass stopped them to say they had missed them at Mass. Mrs. Garcia told them about Espie's singing to God. Everybody looked so pleased, Espie wondered if they thought she was on her way to sainthood.

There were a few people in church, but Espie hardly saw them when she went in. What she saw was Rick and Joaquin setting up the microphones and the drums not far from the altar.

"We can't be that close to the altar, can we?" she whispered.

Mrs. Garcia smiled. "It is a good place. You will be nearer to God." Espie didn't move, and Mrs. Garcia nudged her. "Sing loud so I will hear you."

Espie walked toward the setup. This wasn't what she had expected. In fact, she hadn't thought about where she would sing until this morning. Rick smiled. "I've been waiting for you," he said. Joaquin waved and adjusted one of his drums. Georgie came in with a couple of the girls. They looked relaxed. So did Rick and Joaquin. The church was filling up.

Espie whispered to Rick, "I didn't know everybody could see us when we sang."

He looked past her at the people as though he were seeing them for the first time. "You'll get used to them," he said. The other guitarist came in, and he and Rick tuned their guitars together.

Other kids came in. One of the girls glanced at her watch. "Isn't Allison coming?" she whispered to Espie.

Espie shrugged and tried not to look toward the pews she knew were now almost full. Rick whispered, "Okay, let's get in position." Everybody eased around each other, and Rick motioned to Espie to come stand beside him.

Allison brushed past her and almost knocked over a microphone on the way to her place. The sacristy bell rang, and Rick gave the signal to begin. " 'We three kings of Orient are . . .' " There was none of the dancing in place Espie saw Friday. She heard voices from the altar and from the pews. The priest and the people were singing. Espie joined in on the chorus and hoped nobody could hear her.

The group started together on the second chorus, and Rick smiled at the one sound of "born." When the song ended, the priest said, "In the name of the Father, and of the Son, and of the Holy Spirit." Espie made the sign of the cross with everybody else, and the Mass started. The group answered some of the priest's prayers with song, and although Espie didn't know the melody, she mouthed the words that had become familiar to her through years of going to Sunday Mass.

When the priest approached the pulpit to deliver the sermon, the group sat on folding chairs lined against the wall. Espie glanced at Mrs. Garcia. She smiled, and Espie looked away, more aware than ever of the hundreds of

69

people. She sneaked a look at Allison. Her hands moved nervously. Sometimes they shook, and she forced them still. But she sat straight and beautiful in a pink dress and jacket. If she'd had anything to drink after she hung up last night, she must have slept it off. Her eyes were on the priest, and Espie looked at him too. But she couldn't concentrate on what he was saying. She was too aware of Rick sitting beside her.

After the sermon and the recitation of the Creed, the group sang "Turn, Turn, Turn." Espie wondered what Mrs. Garcia thought about hearing a song that wasn't a regular church hymn, but Espie didn't glance at her until they started the Our Father. People all around Mrs. Garcia were singing, but she stared at the group, her mouth open as though she had started to sing and never got further than "Our." Espie knew she'd hear about it after Mass.

Every member of the group went to Communion, and Espie tagged along so she wouldn't be standing in front of everybody by herself. They were the first to receive the Hosts, and when they got back to their places, Rick whispered to Espie, "We're going to sing 'Prayer of St. Francis.' Fake it." He gave the signal, and the group sang. By the time Mass finished, and they had sung "Go Tell It on the Mountain," Espie felt more religious than she had since the day she made her first Communion.

Most people were out of church by the time the group sang the last line of "Go Tell It on the Mountain." When they finished, Rick said, "You did great. Sorry about springing that Communion song on you, but the group knows it so well, I didn't think about practicing it Friday night." Mrs. Garcia started toward them.

"I never heard it before," Espie told him. "Maybe you

could come to the house and help me learn it."

"Sure, when?"

"How about tomorrow night?"

Rick frowned. "I have to give a guitar lesson tomorrow night. How about Wednesday night?" Mrs. Garcia was beside them now and Espie introduced them.

She told Mrs. Garcia, "Rick said he can come to the house and help me with the songs Wednesday night."

Mrs. Garcia smiled. "I am glad."

Joaquin had been taking down the mikes. He said, "Hey, Rick, if you don't help me, we won't be out of here before the next Mass."

"I'm coming," Rick told him. He asked Espie, "Six thirty okay?"

"Yeah, great. I'll see you Tuesday at rehearsal," Espie told him.

Rick turned to Mrs. Garcia. "It's nice meeting you."

"It is nice for me too," Mrs. Garcia said, and Espie followed her to the door after a wave to Rick.

Allison was waiting for them outside. "Can I give you a ride home?" she asked.

Mrs. Garcia accepted before Espie could say no. She ignored Allison on the way to the Firebird, but Mrs. Garcia asked her, "How long the group sing the Our Father like that?"

"I don't know. They were singing it that way when I joined. Rick wrote the music. He's written a lot of songs."

Allison unlocked the door and walked around the car while Espie hopped in back and Mrs. Garcia sat in front. Allison got in, and Mrs. Garcia said, "The music is so fast, I do not think God is happy."

Allison started the car. "How can God help but be happy when the music is so happy?" she asked.

Mrs. Garcia didn't answer. Espie knew she was thinking that one over. "I do not think He like it. I will talk to Father Acosta about it."

Espie remembered what Rick had said about little old ladies running to the priest. She hoped Father Acosta wouldn't tell Rick who had complained.

Mrs. Garcia asked Allison, "Your mother and father no come to Mass?"

"They had to be in Balboa by ten. A friend of my father's is having a party on his yacht."

"Then you have menudo with us," Mrs. Garcia said. Espie wondered if Mrs. Garcia had caught the word "yacht."

Allison asked, "What's menudo?"

"It's the soup of our people," Mrs. Garcia told her.

"It's supposed to be good for hangovers," Espie said, and saw Allison grip the steering wheel.

Mrs. Garcia smiled. "That is what they say, but our people eat it after Sunday Mass like their parents did it before them. You stay and have some with us?"

Allison stopped in front of Mrs. Garcia's house. "I'd like to do that," she said.

When they got inside, Espie went to the kitchen for the pan she or Denise used every Sunday to carry the menudo from the store. She was halfway out the door when Allison said, "Where you going?"

"To get the menudo."

"I didn't know you went out for it. I'll go with you."

When they got outside, Allison headed for her car. Espie said, "We can walk. It's only up the street."

They turned the corner and a couple of men whistled. One of them said, "Pretty girls. Pretty girls, make love to me."

Espie gripped the handle of the menudo pan and tried

to ignore them. Allison looked scared. "You get used to them," Espie told her.

"Does this go on all the time?"

Espie nodded. "They're wetbacks, just in from Mexico, and they're full of macho stuff."

Espie went in the store, and Allison said, "They scare me."

"You get used to them," Espie said again.

The woman in the store said, "You're late this morning, Espie." She took the pan. "Same as always?"

Espie nodded. Being in the place always made her hungry. Enchilada and taco sauces, chiles, tamales, tortillas—the odors blended and filled the place. The woman gave the pan back to Espie. She paid her and turned to leave. A man carrying an empty pan bumped into her. She held on to her full one. "Excuse me," the man said in Spanish.

Espie said, *"De nada,"* and went out.

Allison told her, "I know what that means. It means, it's nothing."

"It would have been something if the menudo spilled on my dress," Espie said, ignoring the wetbacks they passed.

"Do you really think Joaquin likes me?" Allison asked.

"He looks like he does."

"Then why won't he ask me to go out?"

"Maybe he's afraid you'll say no."

"Why would I?"

"You're Anglo."

"I wouldn't turn him down because he's Mexican."

"How about your folks?"

"What do you mean?"

"Would they let you go with him?"

"Sure, why not?"

"If they don't like to drive through our barrio, they might not like you going out with a Mexican."

"My folks aren't like that," Allison said. She glanced at Espie. "At least my father isn't."

When they got in the house Mrs. Garcia had the bowls on the table. Espie put menudo in each dish, and Mrs. Garcia turned tortillas over the gas flame to warm them. She wrapped them in a clean dish towel and put them on the table.

Espie took one, then squeezed a piece of lemon over her soup. "Want some lemon?" she asked Allison.

"I don't know. I never tasted menudo."

Mrs. Garcia said, "Try it with no lemon and see if you like it."

Allison put a spoonful of soup in her mouth and swallowed. "This is great the way it is."

Mrs. Garcia smiled. "I eat it always without lemon."

While they ate, they talked about the Celebration Group before the subject turned to Denise. Mrs. Garcia said, "Why you no come to the hospital with us? Then you can meet Denise."

"I don't know. I have a lot of things to do."

"Like what?" Espie asked, her voice so tight that Mrs. Garcia looked at her curiously.

"You will like Denise. And she will like you," Mrs. Garcia said.

"You really think so?" Allison asked.

"Come with us. You will see."

Espie watched Allison. Finally, she said, "I guess I can go."

"Good," Mrs. Garcia said. She put her dish in the sink. "You like the menudo?"

"It's delicious. What's in it?" Allison asked.

"Hominy and tripe," Mrs. Garcia told her.

"What's tripe?"

"The inside of a cow's stomach," Espie said. Allison

74

stared at her empty bowl. She looked like she was going to throw up. "Haven't you ever eaten tripe?" Allison shook her head. "We have it a lot," Espie said, and put the lemon in the refrigerator. No need to tell her they ate it because it was cheap, not good—except in menudo.

On the way to the hospital Mrs. Garcia kept saying how glad Denise would be to see Allison, and as she moved into the traffic of the Golden State Freeway, she looked like she believed it. But when they got out of the Firebird in the parking lot of County General, Espie saw her tremble. "I don't like hospitals," Allison told her.

"Neither does Denise," Espie said.

CHAPTER 9

When they reached Denise's bed, Mrs. Garcia started to introduce Allison, but Denise interrupted her. "She's in my English class, remember?"

Mrs. Garcia smiled, "That is right. I forget."

Allison asked, "How do you feel?"

"I've felt better," Denise told her, her voice tight.

"The accident wasn't my fault."

"I know. Officer Parks told me. I'm sorry about your boyfriend." Denise's voice softened a little.

"He wasn't my boyfriend. I mean, he was just somebody I knew." Espie was surprised to see tears spring into Allison's eyes. "That doesn't make it easier to take," she said.

Espie hated downers. She changed the subject. "Rick said he'll come to the house Wednesday to help me learn the Celebration Group songs," she told Denise.

Mrs. Garcia said, "He is a nice boy to do that." Denise glanced at Espie, and Espie winked.

They talked about the Celebration Group, but Allison didn't join in the conversation and answered Denise's questions about the kids in their English class with only a few words or a nod of her head. Mrs. Garcia sat in the only chair, and Espie leaned against the wall, her thumbs in the belt loops of her jeans. But Allison stood rigid at the foot of the bed as though she didn't want anything between her and the door. Her body loosened only when Mrs. Garcia hugged Denise and said it was time to leave.

Denise said, "You don't have to take a bus. Can't you stay longer?" Espie saw Allison stiffen up again.

Mrs. Garcia looked past the bed at the food wagon. "We already stay longer, and now it is time for your supper."

Espie said, "Maybe Allison will drive us down a couple of nights this week. How about it, Allison?"

Allison averted Denise's eyes the way she'd done since they had come in. "I don't think I can. See, my folks don't let me drive the car at night."

Espie said, "You go to the Celebration Group."

"That's different. It's just down the hill." Everybody was looking at Allison. "I'll ask them," she said.

Espie told Denise, "I'll call the Explorers again to make sure they keep coming."

"Thanks."

Allison said, "I hope you won't need the operation."

Espie and Mrs. Garcia stopped moving. "What operation?" Denise's question sounded like a muffled scream. Mrs. Garcia rushed to her.

"Stupid," Espie muttered to Allison.

Denise screamed questions while Mrs. Garcia tried to calm her. A nurse hurried to the bed. "What's the matter?"

"I'm not having an operation."

Denise couldn't move the lower part of her body very much, but the rest of her jerked in every direction. The nurse grabbed her arms and held them, but Denise broke away. Another nurse came. Together they pinned Denise down. "What happened?" the first nurse asked.

Mrs. Garcia said, "It is terrible. Allison say something about the operation."

Denise yelled, "Let me go."

The first nurse said, "We'll let go if you promise to calm down before you hurt yourself."

Denise looked at her legs. "I *am* hurt." Her muscles looked ready to snap. The nurses didn't ease up. Denise stopped fighting, and the women let her go.

Mrs. Garcia moved past them, and Denise buried her face in the woman's arms and sobbed.

Espie looked away. Allison was gone.

It took a long time to explain things to Denise and calm her enough to allow Espie and Mrs. Garcia to leave. When they got in the hall Mrs. Garcia leaned against the wall. Espie asked, "You okay?"

Mrs. Garcia nodded. "Why Allison say that?"

"I guess she didn't know it was a secret from Denise."

"Where she go?"

"To the car, I guess."

"We go. I am very tired."

Espie walked beside her to the parking lot. The Firebird was gone. Espie swore. Mrs. Garcia said, "That will not help."

"Sorry."

Mrs. Garcia rested against a station wagon. "We will take the bus." She took a deep breath and started toward the bus stop. Espie wanted to beat the hell out of Allison.

The moment they got in the house, Espie dialed Allison's number. "Why did you say that to Denise?" she asked when Allison picked up the phone.

"I didn't know nobody told her about the operation."

"You hardly said anything all the time we were there. Why did you have to say anything on the way out? Especially that."

"I guess I wanted her to know I cared about what happened to her."

Espie looked toward Mrs. Garcia's room, where she had gone to lie down. "You could have waited for us."

"I had to get home."

"Yeah, I know," Espie said, and slammed down the receiver.

She started for her room. Mrs. Garcia called from her bed. "What Allison say?"

Espie went to the door of Mrs. Garcia's room. "She said she left because she wasn't feeling well."

"I hope she will feel better."

"She will," Espie said, and went to her room.

The next morning she was a couple of blocks from school when Allison stopped beside her and honked the horn. "Sorry I'm late. Get in."

"No thanks," Espie said, and kept walking.

Traffic was heavy, and Allison had to move the car. But she was waiting for Espie when she got to school. "You don't have to be so mad," Allison said through the open window. Espie didn't even look at her on her way to the gym.

The Firebird wasn't around after classes, and Espie walked home, glad to be rid of her.

Carlos called a few minutes before five. "Old man Gomez finally gave me a night off. Want to go see Denise with me?" he asked.

"Sure."

"How about Mrs. Garcia?"

"She's not home yet, but she'll want to go."

"I'll pick you up at six, okay?"

"Great. We'll be ready."

Mrs. Garcia looked exhausted when she came in, and she was out of breath. The trips to the hospital were getting to her, and Espie wondered how long Mrs. Garcia could keep going. She took off her sweater and headed for the kitchen. Espie said, "I fixed tostadas."

"You are a good girl, Espie," Mrs. Garcia said, and Espie heard the relief in her voice. "Now I can rest."

"Carlos is going to see Denise tonight. He said we could go with him."

Espie took the tostadas out of the oven and put chopped lettuce and tomatoes on them.

Mrs. Garcia slumped in a chair. "I am so tired."

"Then don't go. You were with her all afternoon, and Carlos and I will stay with her as long as they let us."

"Do you think Denise will be sad if I do not go?"

"She'll understand," Espie said, and took a bite from her tostada. "Did you see the doctor?"

"He say Denise will not need the operation, but . . ." Mrs. Garcia shrugged and stared at her food.

"But what?"

"He say it will be a long time before she walks, and he does not know if she will walk right."

"I thought if she didn't need the operation she'd be okay."

"He say she need ther— I do not know the word, but somebody must move her legs until she can move them herself. Then she will have to learn to walk."

"How could she forget how to walk?"

"Her head no forget, but her legs must be taught how to move. I do not understand." She pushed the food away. "You are a good girl to cook the supper, but I cannot eat now." She stood up. "You tell Denise I see her tomor-

80

row," she said, and went to her room. Espie had never seen Mrs. Garcia look so tired or sound so discouraged. She finished her tostada, but she couldn't eat the second one. She wrapped it up with Mrs. Garcia's two and put them in the refrigerator.

She went to Mrs. Garcia's room. It was dark except for the light that flickered from the candle in front of the statue of Our Lady of Guadalupe. "You okay?" Espie asked Mrs. Garcia.

"I am only tired."

Espie went to her room and brushed her hair. When she passed Mrs. Garcia's room on the way to the front door, Mrs. Garcia was gasping. Espie ran in. "What's the matter?"

"It is hard for me to breathe. I will sit up, and it will be easier."

"I'd better stay home."

"I have this before, and always it is better when I sit quiet. You go. I will be fine." She eased her legs to the floor and stood up. "I sit in the living room. Then I can watch television."

Espie walked beside her until she reached the chair. "Want KMEX?" Mrs. Garcia nodded. Her breath was still short and noisy, but she was breathing more normally. Espie turned on the television. "You sure you're okay?"

Mrs. Garcia nodded. "I tell you. I have this before."

Espie heard a car stop and looked out. "Here's Carlos. I'll be back by eight thirty."

"Do not tell Denise I no feel well," Mrs. Garcia said just before Espie closed the door.

Espie hadn't seen Carlos since the night of the accident. He smiled as she approached the car and reached over to open the door. "Where's Mrs. Garcia?"

"She's sick."

Espie closed the door, and Carlos pulled away from the curb. "What's the matter with her?"

"She has trouble breathing."

"She got a cold?"

"No, she just can't breathe. I think the trips to see Denise are too much for her."

"That hill from the bus to the hospital is tough on somebody with asthma."

"Asthma?"

"You know, it makes it hard for people to breathe."

"I know, but Mrs. Garcia doesn't have asthma."

"She doesn't talk about it, but she called my mother a couple of times to go to the clinic with her when the attacks got too bad. My mother's afraid one of these days an attack will put too much strain on Mrs. Garcia's heart."

Espie felt a chill run over her. She huddled in her coat. She hadn't thought about Mrs. Garcia's age or about her getting sick. "Does Denise know?"

"I don't think so. Mrs. Garcia hasn't had an attack for a long time," Carlos said as he eased into the traffic of the Golden State Freeway.

They were almost at the hospital when Espie told him what had happened when Denise found out about the operation the day before.

"What was Allison doing at the hospital, anyway? I'd think she wouldn't want to see Denise when she was in the car that put her there."

"She didn't want to go, but Mrs. Garcia asked her."

"She could have said no."

"Did you ever try to say no to Mrs. Garcia?"

Carlos chuckled. "It's not easy," he said as he pulled into the parking lot.

Denise greeted them with a surprised smile. Her eyes

were dry, but Espie saw she'd been crying. "I didn't know you were coming. Where's Mrs. Garcia?"

"She was too tired to come, but she said she'd see you tomorrow," Espie told her.

Denise said to Carlos, "Mr. Gomez has sure been working you hard."

"I'm not complaining. I used the extra money to buy a tire. And I need another one."

Espie asked Denise, "What's the matter?"

Tears filled Denise's eyes, and she brushed them away. "I don't know. I've been crying on and off since Mrs. Garcia left."

Espie said, "You should be happy. Mrs. Garcia said you don't need an operation."

Anger dried the tears. "Why didn't you tell me about that operation?" She didn't give Espie a chance to answer. "Some friend you are. What else are you hiding from me?"

"Nothing. And I didn't tell you about the operation because the doctor said not to."

"Well, he should have told me something instead of giving me all that double-talk I didn't understand." Tears started again.

"Are you crying because everybody was trying to keep you from worrying about something that might not happen?"

"I'm crying because I want to get out of here." She took a Kleenex from a box on the table by the bed and blew her nose. "They started the therapy," she said.

Espie said, "Therapy. That's the word Mrs. Garcia couldn't remember."

Carlos asked, "What did they do?"

"A couple of women moved my legs. They said it's to keep the muscles from shrinking." Denise hit the bed with her fist. "Damn it, I can't even move my own legs." The quiet tears gave way to sobs.

Espie didn't know what to do, and Carlos looked embarrassed. Espie asked, "How long are they going to keep moving your legs?"

"A few days, then I have to go to the therapy room for exercises and whirlpool baths."

Carlos said, "I saw that room when I took the Explorers' advanced first-aid course. They've got all kinds of equipment. They'll have you walking in no time."

Denise brightened. "Think so?"

Carlos nodded. "The people who work there are terrific."

Denise didn't look convinced, but the tears had stopped again, and after Carlos told her more about the therapy room, they talked about Rick and about the Explorers until a voice announced over the loudspeaker that visiting hours were over.

Denise told Espie, "Don't tell Mrs. Garcia I've been crying." Tears filled her eyes again.

Carlos said, "I'll come back as soon as I can."

"I promise I won't do any crying, okay?"

Espie asked, "Anything you want me to tell Mrs. Garcia?"

"Just that I'm all right." Denise wiped away the tears that spilled down her cheeks. "I hope I dry up before she comes tomorrow."

In the car, Espie said, "She sure was down."

"I'd be down too if I had to face that therapy."

"What do you mean?"

"I've seen people take weeks of therapy just to be able to walk a few steps."

"She won't have to do that, will she?"

"It depends how bad the injury is."

"Why didn't you tell her that?"

"I didn't want her to quit before she starts."

"What do you mean, quit?"

"Some people get so discouraged they quit trying."

"Denise won't do that."

Carlos didn't say anything, and they drove the rest of the way in silence.

When Espie got home, a man's voice coming from the television was talking about unemployment in the barrio. Mrs. Garcia didn't look up. Espie went closer. Mrs. Garcia sat unmoving, her eyes closed.

Espie stopped. "Mrs. Garcia," she said, suddenly afraid to move closer. The woman didn't budge. Espie took a couple of steps toward the chair. "Mrs. Garcia?" she repeated, but the woman still didn't answer. "Mrs. Garcia," Espie screamed, and the woman jumped.

"Espie, what is the matter?"

Espie began to shake. "You didn't answer me. I thought . . . I mean, when I left you could hardly breathe, and I come home and you're so still, I . . ." She sank to the couch. "I'm sorry I scared you."

The man on television stopped talking, and a station break replaced him. Mrs. Garcia said, "I am fine. I tell you I have this before, and always I am fine after I rest."

"Carlos told me . . ." She stopped, and Mrs. Garcia leaned forward, waiting for her to go on.

When she didn't, Mrs. Garcia asked, "What Carlos tell you?"

Espie pushed her hair behind her shoulders. "He said to tell you he hopes you feel better."

Mrs. Garcia smiled and asked, "How is Denise?"

"She's okay. A couple of women started the therapy after you left."

"What they do?"

"They moved her legs to keep the muscles from shrinking. She'll be going to the therapy room in a couple of days for exercises," Espie said, and started for her room because she didn't want to tell Mrs. Garcia what Carlos said about how long it might take for Denise to walk again.

Mrs. Garcia turned off the television and came to the bedroom door to say good night. Espie got her pajamas from under her pillow. "Good night," she said, and pulled off her T-shirt. She was in bed before Mrs. Garcia turned off the light in her room.

Espie lay in the darkness and tried to hear the woman's breathing, but she couldn't. She held her breath and listened—still no sound. She laughed at herself. She had never been able to hear Mrs. Garcia breathing from her bedroom.

Espie turned over and tried to sleep, but she was too worried. If anything happened to Mrs. Garcia, could Mary Parks find Espie another foster home, or would she have to go to juvenile hall because there wasn't anybody to take care of her?

She wondered what Denise would do. It would be hard to find a home for a cripple. But Denise wouldn't be crippled. She'd do anything the therapy people told her to do so she'd get better. Denise was like that. A car passed by. Its lights lit up the room. Espie rolled over on her back. She wondered how often Denise had cried since she'd been in the hospital because she was scared. She had asked Espie not to tell Mrs. Garcia. And Mrs. Garcia had told Espie not to tell Denise about the asthma attack. That left her alone to worry about both of them.

She thought about Rick. She could hardly wait until the Celebration Group rehearsal tomorrow so she could be with him. She sat up and hugged her knees. Damn, she wouldn't be able to go to rehearsal if Allison didn't take her. She'd have to call her in the morning and give her a line about how sorry she was for walking away from her this morning.

She lay back down and tried to push everything from her mind, but things tumbled together. "Don't tell Mrs. Garcia I've been crying" . . . "Do not tell Denise I no feel well" . . . "My mother's afraid one of the attacks will put too much strain on Mrs. Garcia's heart" . . . Espie heard Allison's pleas for help. She saw Rick's wink and his smile. And she saw juvey.

She pulled the blanket over her head to shut everything out. But it didn't help. People needed her help. She didn't like that. She needed their help. She didn't like that, either.

CHAPTER 10

Mrs. Garcia looked okay and was breathing normally when she woke Espie. Espie hadn't slept well, and she was tired. But she crawled out of bed without an argument and headed for the bathroom to take a shower. When she finished, she went to the phone to call Allison. She dialed the first two numbers, then replaced the receiver. Allison might hang up on her. Espie had to have a good reason to make the call. She picked up the phone again. She'd tell her Denise wouldn't need the operation.

Mrs. Summers answered the phone, and Espie asked to talk to Allison. "One moment, please."

She was gone so long Espie thought Mrs. Summers had forgotten her, but Allison finally said a muffled hello.

"I've got great news," Espie told her.

"What?" Allison asked. She sounded like it hurt to talk.

"Denise won't need the operation."

"Is she coming home?"

"Not for a while. But isn't it great about the operation?"

"I thought you just said she didn't need an operation."

"That's what I did say." Allison sounded so confused she had to be coming down from a drunk, but Espie didn't say anything about it. "You going to pick me up?" she asked.

"For what?"

"School."

"Oh, yeah, school." Her voice sounded more alert. "I don't think I can make it. I think I've got the flu or something."

Espie felt like hanging up, but she wanted to go to the Celebration Group rehearsal. "Gee, that's rough." She lowered her voice so Mrs. Garcia wouldn't hear. "You won't be able to see Joaquin."

"Joaquin?"

"It's Tuesday."

"Tuesday?" Espie felt like she was listening to an echo.

"Sometimes when you get up with a cold or something, you feel lousy, but after you start moving around, you feel better. Maybe it would help if you went to school."

Espie knew if Allison was alone, she'd drink all day, and she'd never get to rehearsal. "You already sound better than you did when you came to the phone. Why don't you try going to school? I bet you'll feel well enough tonight to see Joaquin."

"Maybe you're right. But don't wait for me. I'll see you at school."

"Okay, but Allison, don't . . ." Espie stopped.

"Don't what?"

"Don't go back to bed, okay?"

"Okay," Allison said, and hung up.

Allison wasn't at school when the bell rang. Espie hung around outside a few minutes, then went in. She really hadn't figured Allison would make it. But Espie caught a glimpse of her coming out of the head between second and third period.

She looked for her during lunch, but she didn't see her.

She was halfway through her sandwich when she spotted her hurrying toward her car. "Hey, Allison, wait," Espie called, but Allison didn't turn around. Espie grabbed her lunch bag and ran after her. "Where you going?" she asked when she got close enough for Allison to hear above the noise of talking, laughing kids.

"Home." She looked scared.

"Why?"

Allison took her car keys out of her purse, and Espie saw an empty whiskey bottle. Allison said, "I didn't drink it. *Cholas* came in the head while I was taking a drink just now. They finished it off."

"You were smart to give it to them." You didn't argue with *cholas*. They were the toughest girls in the barrio, and most of them belonged to gangs.

"I didn't give it to them. They surrounded me and pulled the bottle out of my hand. I was so scared I just stood there and watched them drink my booze." Her hand shook as she unlocked the car door. "I need a drink," she said, and got in.

Espie said, "Wait, I'll go with you." She hopped in, and Allison pulled away, her tires screeching.

It wasn't until they reached Figueroa and headed south that Espie realized she was cutting classes. She used to do it a lot before she came to live with Mrs. Garcia, but she hadn't done it since. She started to tell Allison to take her back to school but changed her mind. She took a bite from her half-eaten sandwich and leaned back in the seat. She deserved a day off.

Allison turned on Monte Vista, then headed up the curved hill of Museum Drive. The night Espie had come up with Carlos to look for the lost kid, the road hung over an awning of lights. Now she saw houses and freeways below her and mountains in the distance. Each curve revealed a different view as they drove along the narrow road protected from mesquite-covered hills by a wooden rail that didn't look strong enough to keep a bicycle from going into the ravines.

"Is that Los Angeles down there?"

"I think so. I don't know. It might be Pasadena. We can even see Glendale from our house."

They climbed a few more minutes before Allison turned into a driveway lined with eucalyptus trees. She switched off the motor, and they were swallowed by silence. Espie saw why Mrs. Summers liked the house. It clung to the edge of the hill and overlooked everything and everybody in every direction.

Allison slipped off her shoes and opened the front door. Espie took a step inside, then pulled her foot back. A small black rug lay near the door, but beyond it a white carpet stretched to every corner. She took off her shoes and went in.

She walked across the room, decorated in black and white, to the window that formed the wall at the other end of the house and looked out. A woman swam in a pool in her yard below. Espie said, "Wouldn't it be great to have a pool and be able to swim anytime you want to?"

"We had a pool in the Valley, but after a while we hardly ever used it," Allison said. She moved toward the back of the bar in the corner.

"We used to do a lot of things together. Now all my folks do is argue about people, money, where to live, anything. They even argue about me." Espie didn't know what to say or even if she was supposed to say anything, so she just stood by the window and listened. "They really went at it about what school I'd go to after we moved here. My mother wanted me to go to this private school in South Pasadena, but my father said I was going to Frank-

91

lin Heights. They sure yelled at each other about that one. My father won. He usually does." Allison poured a drink and put it to her lips.

"Hey, hold it," Espie said.

"If you came here to stop me from drinking, forget it," she said, and swallowed the drink. She filled the glass with water and poured it into the whiskey bottle, then did it again, to replace the liquor she had drunk.

Espie said, "Let's go someplace."

"Where?"

"How about St. Damien's? Maybe we'll see Rick and Joaquin."

"Do you really think Joaquin likes me?"

"I told you he does, and if we go to St. Damien's, maybe we'll see him."

"How can we see him if he's in school?"

"Maybe it'll be his P.E. time and he'll be playing football or something." Espie started toward the door. "Come on. I don't want to wait until tonight to see Rick."

"Okay, let's go."

Allison hit a holly bush on the way out of the driveway. She put the car in drive, and Espie buckled her seat belt. Several times the car edged close to the rail that lined the hill. Once it swayed to the wrong side of the street, but Allison brought it back.

"Think we'll see Joaquin?" she asked.

"We might if we live through this ride."

Allison laughed. "There's never any traffic up here at this time." A car came around the curve and passed within inches of them. "Well, hardly ever," Allison said.

Traffic was light on Monte Vista when they turned off Museum Drive, and Espie relaxed. They were heading west on San Fernando Road when she saw two policemen talking to a couple of kids. She ducked and came up only when she knew they'd passed them.

"What's the matter?" Allison asked.

"That was Gary Horton and Ron Peters. If they saw me, they'd know I was cutting classes."

"What would they do? Send you to jail for life?"

"No, but they'd take me back to school. There's a sweep on."

"What's a sweep?"

"House-burglary reports during the day jumped so high last month, the Chief told the guys on duty to stop and question juveniles on the streets during school hours. If they don't have a good reason to be out, the cops take them to school and notify their parents."

"That's supposed to stop burglaries?"

"The last time they had a sweep, daytime burglaries dropped twenty-five percent."

Allison glanced at her. "You like being an Explorer?"

Espie nodded. "I didn't think I would, but I do."

They passed a sign that said ST. DAMIEN and approached a high stone wall. "This it?" Allison asked.

"I guess so," Espie said, and Allison stopped the car. They stared at the wall.

Allison said, "We can't even see the school from here. How can we see Joaquin?"

"I guess we won't. I thought they'd have a fence around their P.E. field like Franklin Heights does and we could watch them work out."

"It was a dumb idea," Allison said, and started the engine.

"Let's walk around. Maybe we'll see their cars."

"They don't have cars."

"What were they driving the other night at rehearsal?"

"Their fathers' cars."

Espie said, "Let's go. Maybe there's a fence on the other side and they'll be out for P.E."

Allison shrugged and cut the engine. Espie got out. She hadn't expected to see Rick and Joaquin when she suggested they come. But she had to keep Allison away from her house and that liquor bar until her mother got home.

They followed the wall halfway around the block, but they didn't hear anybody. At Franklin Heights, somebody was always on the field playing football or running track.

Allison repeated, "It was a dumb idea."

"I guess it was. But we'll see them tonight." Espie headed back to the car. "Let's go to my house and watch television. Mrs. Garcia's at the hospital, and we can kill the rest of the afternoon."

"Okay, but let's stop for a bottle first. I'll get some wino to buy it for us."

Allison took her wallet out, and Espie got in the car. "No way. I'd be kicked out of the Explorers and Mrs. Garcia's if I got caught pulling something like that."

Allison threw her wallet back in her purse. "I don't have enough money with me anyway," she said. "Those *cholas* really messed up my day."

As soon as they got to Mrs. Garcia's, Espie turned on the television and watched a soap opera come into view. The actors were sipping drinks while they talked about someone dying and saying nobody should tell the poor guy with the brain tumor that his wife was in love with his doctor. Allison stood up. "Got anything to drink in this house?" Espie shook her head. "What did you do with the bottle you took from me the other night?"

"I threw it away."

"Where?"

"In the trash." Allison headed for the kitchen. "The trash truck came yesterday."

Allison sat down and stared at the television. Espie had seen a lot of kids hooked on drugs, but they didn't look any worse than Allison did now. Espie said, "Maybe you should go to a clinic or something."

"What kind of clinic?"

"I don't know. But there must be someplace you can go to get cleaned up."

"Hey, wait. Guys on skid row go places to get cleaned up. I don't need anything like that. Forget what I said about wanting a drink. I was thirsty, that's all."

"Want some coffee?"

"Yeah, thanks."

Espie went to the kitchen and fixed strong coffee—the way she used to fix it for her mother.

When Mrs. Garcia came in, she said, "Allison, I see your car outside. You study with Espie?"

Espie remembered she had told Mrs. Garcia she would study after school on Tuesdays so she could go to the Celebration Group rehearsal. The television was still on, and there wasn't a book in sight. Ideas raced through Espie's head. Finally she said, "We really lucked out today. We didn't have any homework."

"Nothing?"

"The teachers have conferences after school today and tomorrow. I guess they're making it easy on themselves. How's Denise?" Espie asked all in one breath, and decided the next time she cut classes to have books with her.

"The ladies move her legs again. Dr. Wallace says she has more feelings. He is very happy."

Espie asked, "Did he say how much longer she'd be in the hospital?"

"He does not know." Mrs. Garcia turned to Allison. "You eat with us?"

"No, thank you. I have to go home." Espie had seen Allison's body relax when Mrs. Garcia said the doctor was happy. And she looked relaxed when she told Espie she'd pick her up at six.

"You will not have much time," Mrs. Garcia said.

"I know, but I have to get cleaned up for tonight."

She didn't have the tense look of somebody who needed a drink, and Espie ate the tostada she couldn't eat the night before without worrying about whether Allison would get to rehearsal or not. But when she didn't come at six, and she still wasn't there at six fifteen, Espie figured Allison got boozed up again. But the Firebird stopped in front of the house at six twenty, and Espie ran out. Allison didn't smell of liquor. She didn't even smell of mints.

"I decided to wash my hair. I washed it just before I went to rehearsal the night I joined the group, and Joaquin told me he liked the way it shined."

"That's the nice part of having short hair. You can wash it anytime. It takes hours to dry mine."

"Don't you have a dryer?"

"A lot of people don't."

"Oh," Allison said, as though the idea had never occurred to her.

Rick was giving the group instructions when Espie and Allison came in. Joaquin said, "Hey, Allison, you missed your big chance."

Georgie said, "Yeah, he had to carry his own drums."

Joaquin laughed. "But I'll let you help me carry them out."

Allison smiled and went to stand beside a mike. "I can hardly wait," she said.

Rick told Espie, "I was afraid you weren't coming."

She stood near him. "I had to come. Nobody else knows the songs."

Rick laughed. He looked like he'd rather talk to her than rehearse, but he told the group, "Okay, let's do 'Put Your Hand in the Hand,' " and played the introduction. Espie had heard the song often on the radio and joined in. Rick smiled and did his dance step. Espie was glad she had risked a police sweep to keep Allison sober.

They took a break at seven thirty, and Rick told her, "I wanted to call you yesterday but the odds were against me. Do you know how many Sanchezes there are in the Los Angeles phone book?"

"My number is under my foster mother's name—Garcia."

Rick laughed. "That's as bad as Sanchez," he said. They were in the back of the room, away from the others. Espie noticed Allison stayed with Joaquin instead of taking off for a drink the way she had the week before. Rick didn't ask why Espie lived with a foster mother, and she was glad because she didn't have to say anything about juvenile hall.

"Better tell me where you live so I can find the house tomorrow." Espie told him, and he wrote it down. He glanced at his watch. "I can't give you a ride tonight. My father needs his car by nine o'clock."

"He won't need it tomorrow night, will he?"

"If he does, I'll walk." Rick smiled. "It's okay. He said I could have it tomorrow. Actually, he's pretty good. He lets me use it to come here and whenever the band I play in has a job."

"You play in a band?"

Rick laughed. "You don't have to sound so surprised."

"I didn't mean you weren't good enough. I just don't know anybody who plays in a band. How often do you work?"

"Three or four times a month." He looked at his watch again. "I guess we'd better get back to practice if I'm going to have the car home at nine." He shouted, "Okay, let's do 'Peace, My Friend.' " Everybody moved into place, he gave the signal, and they all began together.

When they finished, Rick walked with his arm around Espie's shoulders to Allison's car. He let her go and opened the door, then leaned down to kiss her. His guitar case hit her leg. He put it down and kissed her hard.

"See you tomorrow night, okay?"

"Okay," Espie said.

She watched him hurry toward his father's car. He turned and waved before he got in.

Tomorrow was going to be a long day.

CHAPTER 11

Allison was in a great mood on the way home. She said she was meeting Joaquin the next night, and she talked about it most of the way to Espie's house. But when she stopped to let Espie out, Allison's mood changed. "Wait for me in the morning. I don't want to face those *cholas* alone."

"They won't bother you if you don't have a bottle."

"You sure?"

"I've been around this hustling since kindergarten. Nobody bothers you after you show them you don't have anything to give them." Espie opened the door.

"I'll get here on time," Allison told her.

"I'll be waiting."

Allison looked tense the next morning, but they talked about Rick and Joaquin most of the way to school, and when they got there Allison told Espie she'd meet her at lunchtime. But Espie saw her heading for the Firebird between third and fourth periods.

"Where you going?"

"I can't take this place. The kids in gym gave me a bad

time because I missed a ground ball. My math teacher started on me the minute I got in the class. And the *cholas* pushed me around." Perspiration formed above Allison's lips. "I can't take the hassling," she said. Her hands shook so much, she had trouble getting the key in the lock.

"Everybody gets hassled sometime."

Allison opened the door. "Well, I can't handle it." She got in and drove away.

When Espie got home, Allison was waiting for her. She hopped out of the car as Espie approached it. "I went home, but my mother's car was in the driveway so I drove around, then came here to wait for you." She looked relaxed, and from the way she held her purse, Espie knew there was a bottle in it.

When they got inside, Espie dropped her books on the couch and sat down. "You know, when I was training at the police academy they told us about something called Alcoholics Anonymous." Espie eased her leg over the arm of the couch. "I was really interested because I figured they might be able to help my mother stop drinking. But the instructor said the A.A. people can't help a drunk until he wants to quit. And my mother didn't want to quit."

"How do they help?"

"I don't know. I quit listening when they said the drinker had to want to stop. But I can find out from Officer Parks after the Explorer meeting tomorrow."

Allison fingered the purse clasp. "Then she'll know I drink."

"I don't have to tell her why I want to know." Espie lowered her foot to the floor. "It's up to you. You've got the problem."

Allison looked at her a long time. "Okay, ask her," she said finally.

Espie glanced at Allison's purse. "You going to keep the bottle?"

"Yeah, well . . ." She stood up. "I have to go home and start getting ready for my date."

Allison went out, and Espie watched her through the window. As soon as she got in the car, she took a long swig from her bottle.

Mrs. Garcia came home a few minutes later. "How come you're home so early?" Espie asked.

"They take Denise to the ther— How you say that word?"

"Therapy."

Mrs. Garcia nodded. "They take her to that room to put her in a bath where the water moves, so I come home."

"What's the bath supposed to do?"

"It will help her muscles, and the women say it is easier for Denise to move her legs in the water."

"How does Denise feel about it?"

"She is happy. She is smiling when I leave." Mrs. Garcia went to the kitchen, and Espie wondered if Denise was still smiling or whether she was crying the way she had cried Monday when Espie and Carlos went to see her.

"I make soup before I leave today. We will have that, then I will clean the kitchen so everything will look nice for when Rick comes."

As soon as Espie finished eating she went to her room to get ready. She had three tops to go with her jeans, and she tried them all on twice. She finally decided on the orange one. That's the one she had on the first time she saw Rick.

She let Mrs. Garcia answer the door, but hurried out of her room as soon as she heard his voice. "Hi Rick, it's great of you to do this."

He came in carrying his guitar case. "I'm glad you're so interested. It's good for the group."

He put his case on the couch and took out his guitar. "Let's try 'Peace, My Friend.' It's going to be our entrance song, and you had trouble with it last night."

Espie had hoped Mrs. Garcia would go to the kitchen and sew, but she stayed in the living room. Espie sat on the couch beside the guitar case. Rick smiled. "You can't sing sitting down." Espie stood up, and he handed her a sheet of paper. "Here're the words. I'll run through the chorus, then we'll try it together." He sang, " 'Peace, I leave with you my friends. Shalom, my peace in all you do. . . .' " Espie looked at Mrs. Garcia. She was watching Rick and keeping time with her fingers. He finished the chorus. "Okay, now try it with me."

He played an introduction and started to sing. She came in in the middle of the first line. When they finished the chorus, he said, "Better come stand by me the way we do in church." Espie glanced at Mrs. Garcia. She looked like she was waiting for more music. Rick played the introduction, and he and Espie went through the chorus again.

They did it a few more times before he went on to the melody. When seven o'clock rang, Mrs. Garcia stood up. "I will go say the rosary. You sing more. When you sing to God it is like the rosary," she said, and went into her room.

Rick looked at Espie. She didn't figure there should be too much silence while Mrs. Garcia was out of the room. "Let me try the melody with you this time."

Rick started, and Espie joined in. She felt the closeness, and from the way he looked at her, she knew he felt it too. They went to the chorus. When they finished Rick kissed her. He winked and smiled. "Okay, let's sing it from the beginning," he said, and his music shut out Mrs. Garcia's Hail Marys.

By the time Mrs. Garcia came back in the room, Rick had switched to the Offertory song, and they practiced that awhile.

At eight thirty he asked Espie, "Had enough?"

"What are we going to do for the Communion song?" Espie asked. She didn't want him to go.

"Father Acosta asked me to do 'Prayer of Saint Francis' again. He likes that one."

"Can we run through it a couple of times? You sprung it on me without any practice, remember?"

Rick grinned. "That's right. Okay, let's try it."

Mrs. Garcia stayed in the room with them and at nine o'clock told them it was time to stop. She thanked Rick for coming and walked with him and Espie to the door. "Rick, why you sing the 'Our Father' so fast?" she asked.

"The kids like it. We have another version, but we haven't sung it for a while."

"I think it is nice if you sing it slow. What you think?"

Rick looked from her to Espie. "It's really hard to sing. The kids know it, but you wouldn't be able to handle it." He looked back at Mrs. Garcia. "I suppose I could come back next Wednesday and we could practice it."

"That will be nice. Then I can learn it too so I can sing with everybody."

Rick opened the door. "I'll see you Sunday at Mass. Good night." He went out and closed the door.

"He is a nice boy," Mrs. Garcia said.

Espie leaned against the door. He's a fast thinker too, she thought.

Espie watched for the Firebird the next day and spotted it a couple of blocks from school. Allison stopped the car, and Espie got in. "Did you talk to Mary Parks?" Allison asked before the door was even closed.

"I told you I'm not going to see her until tonight. How was your date with Joaquin?"

"I got smashed." Her voice was angry. "I just had some drinks. You know, I wanted to get relaxed so I'd have some fun, but I didn't stop drinking soon enough." She looked like she was going to cry.

"I'll talk to Parks," Espie said.

As adviser, Mary Parks sat in on L.E.E.G. meetings, but Captain Alice Eliott ran it with help from her lieutenant and her sergeant. After roll call and dues collection most of the meeting was spent discussing two things Espie was really interested in. The first thing was a schedule so there would be one or two girls with Denise every night during the next week. The second thing was a snow trip to the mountains. Espie had never been to the mountains, and she'd never been in snow. So when Alice called for a vote to find out how many girls wanted to spend the money in the Explorer bank account to go to the mountains, Espie's hand shot up first. More than half the girls voted with her, and they made plans to go at the end of February or the beginning of March. Espie wondered if Denise would be well enough to go.

Espie was still excited about the trip when she sat in Mary Parks's office after the meeting ended.

Parks leaned back in her chair and faced Espie across the desk. "What did you want to talk to me about?"

"I want information on Alcoholics Anonymous." Espie had asked Parks for help before, and she always came through without a lot of questions.

"You learned that at the Academy, didn't you?"

"I heard about it, but I didn't learn it."

Parks grinned. "Well, it's a group of alcoholics who try to help other alcoholics."

"Like how?"

"By helping them stay off booze."

"How do they do that?" Espie thought about Allison. "If somebody wants a drink, he'll get it unless you stand guard over him all the time."

"People in A.A. don't stand guard over anybody because they know they can't make an alcoholic stop drinking. But they talk to him, listen to him, anything, to let the person know he's not alone." Parks picked up a paper clip and bent it open, but she didn't take her eyes off Espie, and Espie knew Parks was trying to figure out why Espie wanted the information. "You know there's a difference between somebody who drinks once in a while and somebody who has to have a drink, don't you?" Espie shrugged. Parks said, "People who have to have a drink are hooked on booze as much as some people are hooked on drugs. They need help to get off the stuff, and Alcoholics Anonymous gives that help."

Espie rolled her hair around her finger. "What does a person have to do to belong?"

"They have to admit they have a drinking problem, and they want to get rid of it."

"That sounds easy."

"Well, it isn't." Parks leaned forward. "You've heard kids say they weren't hooked on drugs, and they could stop taking them anytime they want?" Espie nodded. "It's the same thing for alcoholics. Most of them won't admit they have to have a drink."

"How much does it cost to belong?"

"It's free."

"If somebody wanted to join . . . I mean, suppose somebody wanted to talk to people about this A.A., how could he get in touch with them?"

"The number is in the phone book. Just call, and they'll

105

tell you when there's a meeting and where it is."

Espie pushed her hair behind her shoulders and stood up. "I better go. Carlos is waiting for me."

Parks walked with her to the door. "I'm always here to help," she said.

Espie smiled. "I know. Thanks."

When Espie got home, Mrs. Garcia was sewing. "How is the meeting?" she asked.

"Okay." Espie took off her uniform tie. "We set up a schedule so Denise will have visitors every night."

Mrs. Garcia smiled. "That is nice. I will tell her tomorrow," she said. She looked so tired, Espie wished she could talk her out of going to the hospital every day. She went to her room to undress. She had just gotten her pajamas on when the phone rang.

She hurried out of the room. "I'll get it. It's probably Allison." She picked up the phone. "Hello."

"Espie?"

Espie recognized Rick's voice. "Hi," she said.

"I get out of school at noon tomorrow. Can you meet me?"

"I've got school all day."

"Joaquin called Allison, and she said she'd meet him at one o'clock in Lincoln Park. I was hoping you could come with her."

"Sure, I can do that."

"That's great. We'll meet you at the picnic area."

"I'll be there," Espie said, and hung up.

She was surprised that Joaquin had called Allison after she didn't show up for their date. She was going to call her and ask about it, but the phone rang before she picked up the receiver.

Allison said, "I tried to call you but your line was busy. Were you talking to Rick?"

106

"Yes. Hey, how come . . . ?" Espie started but Allison interrupted.

"You going to meet him?"

"Yes. How come Joaquin called you? I figured he'd be mad after last night."

"He was. He called to tell me off, but I told him I was sick and I was really sorry about not showing. He stayed mad for a while, but before we finished talking, he told me about not having any school tomorrow afternoon and I said maybe I could meet him someplace and make up for last night. Did you talk to Mary Parks?" Allison asked suddenly.

Espie didn't want to talk about Alcoholics Anonymous with Mrs. Garcia in the next room. "I'll tell you about it tomorrow."

"What did she say?"

"I'll tell you tomorrow," Espie repeated.

"Tell me now."

"I can't," Espie said, and hung up.

She went to her room and lay across her bed in the dark. She shouldn't have agreed to meet Rick, not with a sweep on. Suppose the police picked her up and took her back to school? Mrs. Garcia would find out she'd ditched classes. And Parks would know.

Ditching was dumb, but she couldn't miss the chance to see Rick. She sat up. She wished Denise was home so they could talk.

CHAPTER 12

The next morning Allison was late as usual, and Espie began to worry. If Allison didn't make it to school, Espie wouldn't be able to get to Lincoln Park unless she hitched a ride. And if she did that, she'd have to cut most of the morning classes because she didn't know how long it would take her to get picked up. Besides, she hated to put out her thumb. She'd had some bad times when she tried to run away to Mexico by hitching.

She huddled in her sweater and swore at Allison. When she finally turned the corner and stopped, Espie jumped in. "Can't you ever be on time?"

Allison ignored the question. "What did Officer Parks say about Alcoholics Anonymous?"

"She said it's a group of alcoholics who help other alcoholics."

"How?" Allison asked, and Espie told her what Parks had said.

When Espie finished, Allison looked disappointed. "What's the matter?" Espie asked.

"I thought they had something to help me quit."

"Like what?"

"I don't know. Just something. But what kind of help is admitting I've got a problem?"

"And wanting to quit," Espie said.

"I don't know. I don't want to talk to a bunch of drunks."

Espie didn't say another word. Allison still didn't believe she was a drunk.

They left school at lunchtime and stopped at a gas station to ask directions to the park. As soon as they pulled out, Allison said, "Let's get a bottle."

"Forget it," Espie told her.

"Maybe Joaquin and Rick would like a couple of drinks."

Traffic was light as they drove from school at lunchtime, and Espie kept her eyes open for police cars. "Did you ever figure there's millions of people out there who don't need a couple of drinks in the middle of the day?"

"Well, I do, and there's the guy who'll get them for me," Allison said, pointing to a man searching through a trash basket.

She stopped the car and was outside before Espie could stop her. She started after her, then decided to stay in the car. She could duck down in the car, but there wasn't anyplace to hide outside. She watched Allison open her purse as she approached the man. When he looked up, she was holding the money for him to see. Within seconds he shuffled off to the liquor store on the corner.

Allison hurried to the car. "He'll be back in a couple of minutes."

But the couple of minutes turned to ten, and the man still didn't come out of the store. "What's holding him up?" Allison said. She tapped the steering wheel.

Espie glanced at the clock over the Bank of America. "We'd better get moving or the guys will think we won't show."

Allison opened the door. "I'm going to see what's keeping him." Espie watched for patrol cars, and Allison disappeared into the liquor store.

She was out in a minute and broke into a run. She pulled open the door. "The bastard skipped out the back." She turned on the ignition, and the motor came alive. The tires squealed as she pulled out. "I'm going to find him. That's all the money I had," she said, and turned the corner.

"He's long gone. Let's go meet the guys."

"I'm going to find him," Allison repeated, but although they cruised the area three times, they didn't see him. Allison swore and headed toward Lincoln Park. She was still swearing at the wino when they got there.

Espie saw a couple of tables a short way down the tree-lined street. "They're not there," she said.

They drove past the tables and followed the curve in the road. Allison said, "There they are."

Rick and Joaquin waved and hurried to the car. Rick said, "We thought you changed your mind."

Espie looked at Allison. "We got hung up," she said. She eased out of the car and saw more tables behind the bushes.

A guy jogged past them, his clothes and face wet with perspiration. Joaquin said, "That's the second time he comes by here. Must be some kind of a nut." Allison didn't get out of the car, and Joaquin sat in the seat Espie had just left. "I really like this car," he said.

Allison asked, "Want to go for a ride?"

He leaned back in the seat. "Anyplace you say."

"Let's go to my house," Allison said.

110

Joaquin looked at Allison. "You mean it?"

"Sure. We can play records and stuff."

Joaquin grinned. "What's stuff?"

Allison smiled. "Anything you say."

Joaquin pulled the seat up. "Okay, you guys, hop in."

Rick glanced at Espie. He didn't look like he wanted to go, and Espie didn't want to ride down that hill again after Allison had hit her folks' bar. "Why don't we just cruise around?" Espie said.

Allison glared at her. "I don't have enough gas for cruising."

Rick said, "I've got a couple of dollars."

Allison said, "Cruising is stupid when there's a sweep on."

Joaquin asked what a sweep was, and Espie told him. He and Rick had never heard of it. Joaquin said, "We're in the clear. We don't have school."

Allison said, "Well, we do, and I say the safest place is my house."

Joaquin was still holding the seat forward. "Come on, let's go."

Espie said, "We can stay here. The police wouldn't waste their time coming through now. It's too quiet." She nodded toward the bushes. "Besides, we can sit back there. If they do come by, they won't even see us."

Allison asked, "Are you getting in?"

Rick said, "Espie's right. We can . . ."

Allison said, "Close the door." And before Joaquin got it shut, Allison had the engine on. He said something, but Espie didn't hear what it was as the car roared away.

"What's bugging her?" Rick asked.

Espie shrugged and started toward one of the tables barely visible behind the bushes. Rick sat opposite her. "Think she'll come back?"

"If she doesn't, I'll be walking home."

"We can take a bus," he said. He smiled. "I'm glad they left."

Three small girls ran past them and climbed on the seats hooked to the next table. Two women followed them, saw Espie and Rick, and told the children they could eat at the table near the swings. The girls jumped up and went with their mothers.

Rick smiled. "Nice kids."

"Nice mothers," Espie said.

"Want to go to a movie tonight?"

"I can't."

"How about next Friday night?" She looked at him. "It's the first night I've got free. The band has a job tomorrow and Sunday. And I have to give a music lesson Monday night." He smiled. "I know, let's go to a movie Wednesday instead of practicing the songs for the Celebration Group."

"Mrs. Garcia wouldn't go for that."

"She worried about you knowing the songs? You'll pick them up during regular practice."

"That's not it. She's just strict about dating."

"My folks are like that with my sister, but they let her go to a movie with a guy if they think he's nice." Rick frowned. "Doesn't Mrs. Garcia like me?"

"She wouldn't let you come to the house if she didn't."

"Then what's the problem?"

"She worries a lot. See, she's responsible for me." It was warm and quiet. The bushes cut off everything else. And although they sat across from each other, Espie felt really close to him. She decided to tell him about juvenile court.

When she finished, he said, "You haven't been out with a guy since you went to live with her?" Espie shook her

112

head. "That's not normal." He said it with such shock they both laughed.

"It hasn't been bad. I've been busy with the Explorers and . . ." She decided not to say anything about how she used to see Carlos a couple of times a week at Explorer activities or at the house. "It just hasn't mattered until now." He leaned across the table and kissed her. "I'll talk to her about it tonight," Espie said, and kissed him back.

They took the bus home, glad Allison didn't come back for them. And when they reached Espie's stop, Rick got off with her. But she only let him walk with her for a couple of blocks. "Mrs. Garcia should still be at the hospital, but . . ." She shrugged. "I don't want to take any chances. If she saw us together, she'd figure I'd ditched school." He held her hand. "I'll talk to her as soon as she gets home." She pulled away slowly and started down the street. When she turned, he was still watching her. She waved and kept walking.

Espie thought of what she'd say to Mrs. Garcia and decided to talk about the Celebration Group during supper and let the conversation move to going out with Rick. But when Mrs. Garcia came home, she was having trouble breathing, and she said she didn't want any supper. She went to lie down while Espie warmed up some soup for herself.

Before she finished eating, Mrs. Garcia got up from the bed and went to sit in the living room. But it didn't help her to breathe easier. Espie rinsed off her plate and switched on the television. She couldn't concentrate on the program. She wanted to talk about Rick, but Mrs. Garcia's breathing kept her from bringing up the subject. She stared at the picture and waited.

Allison called at eight. "You know what my mother

113

did?" Her words were slurred and angry. "She came home early with a headache and kicked Joaquin out. She called him a dirty Mexican and kicked him out." Allison was shouting now. And Espie knew she was crying.

"Hey, calm down."

"Do you know what Joaquin said when she called him a dirty Mexican?" Allison chuckled. He said, 'Mrs. Summers, I must have gotten dirty in your house because I was clean when I left mine.' Then he left. He walked out the door, and I'll never see him again." Allison was really crying now.

"You'll see him at church Sunday."

"She took my keys, and she won't be back until late Sunday night. She and my father are flying to San Francisco for a convention or something. I'm stuck on this damn hill all weekend." She sniffed into the phone. "It doesn't matter anyway. Joaquin won't talk to me again."

"Of course he will."

"You think so?"

"Sure. He can't blame you for what your mother said."

"He was really mad when he left. Maybe I should call him."

Espie didn't think it was a good idea for Allison to call Joaquin while she was smashed. "Look, there's a couple of hundred Lopezes in the phone book. It would take you all night to find the right one."

Allison said, "I guess you're right. But how can I tell him I'm sorry about what happened?"

"I'll explain things to him Sunday."

"Thanks," Allison said, and sounded a little calmer when she hung up.

At ten o'clock, Mrs. Garcia still had trouble breathing, and she said she was going to try to sleep in a chair instead of going to bed. She was still having problems in the

114

morning, and she asked Espie if she'd mind going to the hospital alone.

Espie thought of Rick. "No, I don't mind."

"That is good. If it is a school day, I go to the hospital so Denise will not be alone, but I let you go today so I can be better tomorrow to go with you."

Espie hurried to her room and brushed her hair while she tried to think of a way to get hold of Rick to ask him to go to the hospital with her. There probably weren't too many Fernandos in the phone book, but she couldn't call from the house with Mrs. Garcia in the living room. And Espie didn't have any money except the money she'd get for the bus. She wished they could have talked about Rick last night.

She went to the phone book and checked out the listings for Fernando. Two of them were close enough to her house to be the right one. It didn't matter if she used ten cents or twenty cents to find Rick. If she spent any of the bus money, she'd have to hitch a ride or walk a couple of miles to a change-of-fare zone. But if she got the right number, Rick would meet her, and he'd have money to make up what she spent on the calls so she wouldn't have to walk.

She brought Mrs. Garcia her purse. "I'll need bus money," she said.

"You leave now? It is too early."

Espie thought of the couple of miles' walk. "I know, but I haven't seen Denise all week. I want to get there when visiting hours start so we'll have plenty of time to talk."

"I will be fine. You go, and do not worry."

Espie went out and half-ran, half-walked to the phone booth at the corner of Broadway and Daly. She opened the phone book and tried to decide which number to dial first. She looked at the other names again and thought that one more number could be the right one. If she used thirty cents, she'd have to hitch a ride most of the way, because she wouldn't have enough money even from the change-of-fare zone.

She stared at the phone and wondered if she should spend the money on the calls. She could be wasting it. But if Rick met her, he could come with her to the hospital. Then they could leave early. Denise would understand, and she'd never tell Mrs. Garcia. It was worth the gamble. Espie took a dime from her pocket and dialed the first number. A woman answered almost right away. "Is Rick there?" Espie asked.

"You have the wrong number. There's no Rick here."

"Wait, don't hang up. Do you know a Rick Fernando?" Espie asked. She figured he could be a relative or something.

"No, I don't. Why don't you check the phone book?"

"Thanks," Espie said, and hung up.

She put another dime in the phone and dialed the next number. "Rick. Answer. Please answer," she said into the phone, and held her breath when she heard the first ring.

CHAPTER 13

Espie let the phone ring a dozen times, reluctant to admit that, if she had dialed Rick's number, she wouldn't reach him because there wasn't anybody home. She hung up finally and heard her dime return. She took the coin, put it back in the phone, and dialed the third number from the book. A man answered and said he didn't know anybody named Rick, but if she told him where she was, he'd be glad to take care of any problems she had. She slammed the phone in his ear.

She stepped out on the sidewalk crowded with people waiting for a bus to go downtown. She thought about asking one of them for twenty cents, but decided against it. She had panhandled a couple of times, and it made her feel like zero, less a couple of points. She started walking and kept her eye out for Rick. If the second number she dialed had been his, he was out someplace. Why not right here on this street? It was dumb. But Mrs. Garcia believed in miracles. Maybe they really did happen. But Espie reached the change-of-fare zone without seeing Rick or anybody else she knew. She sat on the bench at the bus

117

stop and decided miracles didn't happen, but the idea they might was what kept people going.

She got to the hospital late, and Denise said, "I was beginning to think you wouldn't get here. Where's Mrs. Garcia?"

"She's tired. She's been doing a lot of sewing, and she said she was going to rest today and come tomorrow."

"It's been rough on her coming here every day." Denise looked better than she'd looked Monday. The bruise marks were gone, her hair was brushed, and she had lipstick on.

Espie sat down, and Denise said, "Mrs. Garcia told me about the songs Rick taught you Wednesday night. She really likes him. Why don't you bring him here so I can meet him?"

"I almost did that today." Espie told her about trying to call him and about ditching classes the day before.

"Mrs. Garcia would never let you go out with him if she found out about that."

"I know, but I really wanted to see him."

"So, talk to her about it."

"I was going to last night, but she . . ." Espie stopped. "But she was so busy sewing I didn't have a chance," she said so Denise wouldn't worry about the asthma attacks. "How's the therapy coming?" she asked.

"Great. You know, I was really scared. I figured I had to depend on doctors and therapists for everything, but it's not like that. They tell me what to do, but I'm the one who has to do it. And I can do anything I want to if I want to do it bad enough. The therapists say they've never seen such progress." Denise pushed her hair back and smiled. "They haven't seen anything yet."

"How long you going to be here?"

Denise's smile vanished, and tears filled her eyes. "I

don't know. It depends on how things are mending inside of me." She brushed the tears away. "I guess it isn't really all up to me, is it?"

"Have the L.E.E.G.s been coming to see you?" Espie asked because Denise's tears made her feel uncomfortable.

Denise nodded. "They said they're planning a snow trip."

"It isn't definite. You know how long it takes for them to plan things. I can see us heading for the snow in June."

Denise laughed, and Espie didn't see any more tears. She felt good about that on her way home. She felt even better when she found Mrs. Garcia cooking chiles rellenos and breathing normally.

"Shouldn't you be resting?" Espie asked.

"I rest and rest and I feel better so I fix chiles rellenos because you like them. How is Denise?" Mrs. Garcia asked as she took the browned chiles from the hissing fat.

"She's okay. She said the therapy people think she's doing great." Espie put the plates on the table. "She looks better than she did when I saw her Monday."

"I think that too when I go yesterday." Mrs. Garcia sighed. "I will be happy when she can come home."

Espie put salsa colorado on her chiles rellenos. "She's really interested in the Celebration Group. I told her how great the kids are and how hard Rick worked to teach me the songs Wednesday night." Mrs. Garcia took a bite of her food. Espie said, "He asked me to go to a movie next weekend."

Mrs. Garcia stopped eating. "What you tell him?"

"I said I'd ask you if I could go." Mrs. Garcia didn't say anything. Espie said, "Can I go?"

"I do not know him."

"What do you mean you don't know him? He was here Wednesday night."

"I mean I do not know him well. And I do not know his family."

"I'm not asking to marry him. I'm just asking if I can go to a movie with him." Espie's voice was sharp. She knew she wouldn't get anyplace that way. She decided to cool it, but when Mrs. Garcia didn't say anything, Espie said, "You never let me go anyplace."

Mrs. Garcia looked surprised. "You go to the rehearsal Tuesday nights and you go to Explorer meetings. That is going someplace."

"But I don't go out with guys. It's . . . it's not normal," Espie said, remembering the way Rick had kissed her after he said that the day before.

Mrs. Garcia looked hurt. "You are not happy here?"

"I'm happy. I just . . . I just think I should be able to go to a movie with Rick."

"Maybe you are right," Mrs. Garcia said slowly. "I will think about it."

"What's there to think about?"

"Many things." Espie didn't know if she should keep pushing or try again later. She had almost finished the chiles rellenos when Mrs. Garcia said, "When I think about it, I will think I am you and I want to go to a movie with Rick."

Espie wondered if Mrs. Garcia could remember what it was like to be fifteen. She wanted to ask her, but she decided against it. She'd see Rick at rehearsal Tuesday and he was coming to the house Wednesday. Espie didn't want to mess that up.

When she got to church the next morning, Rick whispered, "What did Mrs. Garcia say about the movie?"

"She's thinking about it." Rick looked disappointed.

Joaquin moved closer to them. "Is Allison coming?" he asked. Espie shook her head. "Did she tell you what her mother did Friday?" Espie nodded. "Allison sure belts down the booze, doesn't she?" he whispered.

The kids were getting into place, and Rick told Joaquin to move to his drums. He reached them as the sacristy bell rang. Espie was still nervous about singing where everybody could watch her, but she liked being next to Rick. She glanced at Mrs. Garcia. She was singing with the group. And when the priest began the Mass, Espie prayed that Mrs. Garcia would remember what it was like to be fifteen.

When they got out of church Mrs. Garcia asked Espie why Allison hadn't been in church. "Maybe she's sick," Espie said.

"You should call her when we get home to see." Espie nodded, but she didn't want to talk to Allison. She took longer than usual to go for the menudo and ate it so slowly Mrs. Garcia told her to hurry or they'd never get to the hospital.

They had a great visit with Denise. She had moved one of her legs by herself just before they came in, and she was excited. "Nothing can stop me now," she said, and Espie believed it.

The phone was ringing when they got back home. Espie answered it, and Mrs. Garcia went to her room to rest. Allison said, "If Joaquin asks why I'm not at Mass tomorrow, don't tell him my mother took my car keys with her. Just tell him I'm sick."

"There's no Mass tomorrow. It's Monday."

"You crazy? Tomorrow is Sunday." Her voice had been soft, but now it was angry.

Espie remembered the Summers's fully stocked bar. "Have you been drinking since Friday night?"

"I've had a few. You know, just to keep me company." Her voice was soft again. "If Joaquin says anything about

121

the way my mother acted yesterday, tell him she just wasn't feeling well. And tell him I've got the flu or something, okay?"

Espie was going to tell her again it was Sunday, not Saturday, but decided against it. She figured by the time Allison realized today was Sunday, her folks would be home, and she'd have to watch her drinking. Espie had heard about kids losing days while they went on a drug trip, but she'd never heard of anybody losing a day from drinking. Even her mother knew what day it was when she drank.

Espie started for the kitchen, then turned back to the phone. She looked up the number of Alcoholics Anonymous and dialed.

A man answered, and Espie said, "Somebody told me if I called you, you'd tell me when the next A.A. meeting is."

The man asked, "What area are you in?"

"Do you have to know that?"

"I don't want to know your address. I just want to know the area so I can tell you the location of the meeting closest to you," the man said, and Espie told him what he wanted to know.

"There's a meeting Wednesday night at seven o'clock," he said, and gave her the address.

"If somebody wanted to go there, what would she have to do?"

"Just go."

"Does she have to say who she is?"

"We only use first names, but she doesn't even have to do that."

"Then nobody knows who anybody is?"

"Only if a person wants people to know."

"What do you do there?"

122

"There's different kinds of meetings. The one Wednesday night is the kind where members talk about their drinking problems and how they solved them—or didn't."

"That blows it. This girl would never do that."

"She doesn't have to. Most people just sit and listen."

"I don't know how that can stop anybody from drinking."

"If a person comes to a meeting, he's admitting he has a problem, or at least he's beginning to think he has one. That's an important first step. Then maybe at the meeting he'll hear people tell a lot of stupid things he's been doing and realize he's not alone. That's part of the secret of A.A. If this person is a friend of yours, try to get her to come. I'll always be grateful to the friend who talked me into going to my first meeting."

"You were an alcoholic?" Espie asked, as surprised that he admitted it as she was that he was one.

"I'm a recovered alcoholic. I drank for twenty years. During the last three of those, I drank all day every day. But I haven't had a drink for almost five years."

Espie felt Mrs. Garcia looking at her and realized she had gotten up. "I have to hang up now, Allison. See you at school tomorrow," she said, and put down the phone.

"Allison is sick?"

"She said she's feeling a little better."

"That is nice." Mrs. Garcia started for the kitchen. "I will fix supper."

Espie helped her, and while they worked Espie wondered if A.A. could help Allison. She drank so much. But the man said he used to drink all day. Allison didn't do that. And she'd only been drinking four years. Maybe A.A. was the answer. She'd talk to Allison tomorrow—if she was sober.

CHAPTER 14

Espie didn't see Allison before classes Monday morning. But she saw her going into the counselor's office during lunch period. When Espie spotted her in the hashline, she went to stand beside her. Shouts and whistles exploded from the kids. Espie yelled, "Gag up, I'm not cutting."

The noise died slowly as the kids saw she wasn't breaking into the line. She asked Allison, "When did you get here?"

"Third period."

Allison looked great. Espie couldn't understand it. Her mother looked a wreck after a drinking weekend. Maybe it had something to do with age. They moved slowly to the head of the line. "Your folks get back okay?"

"I was sleeping when they came home, and my mother was sleeping when I left, so I took my car keys out of her purse. But I wish I hadn't."

"Why?"

"The counselor got me. She wants to see my folks because I'm flunking." They reached the head of the line, and Allison bought a hamburger and a Coke.

"Will they come?" Espie asked as they headed toward the wall. A lot of parents didn't.

"I'm not going to tell them."

"They'll know you're flunking when they get your report card in the mail."

"I usually get the mail when I get home. I'll just forge my mother's name." Allison took a sip of her Coke. "Did you see Joaquin at church yesterday?" Espie nodded. "Did he say anything about Friday?"

"We didn't have time to talk much."

"Is he mad?"

"He didn't seem to be, but he sounded surprised at how much you drank Friday."

Allison glanced at her. "I only had a couple of shots."

"I called Alcoholics Anonymous last night."

"Why?"

"I figure you need help."

"I'm making it."

"You were bombed all weekend. I think you should give A.A. a try." The bell rang.

"And I think you're crazy," Allison said, and walked away.

When Espie reached her health class, she saw the movie projector set up in the back of the room. She sat back and relaxed. It was going to be that kind of a period.

The teacher said, "As I told you Friday afternoon"—Espie thought of Rick and Lincoln Park—"we have two films scheduled today. One is on marijuana and one is on alcohol. We talked about the films Friday, and we'll be discussing them all week, so pay attention and take notes. All right, Bob, start the film, please," she said, and switched off the lights.

In the film, nine kids were sitting on the floor. While

125

the title of the film and the names of the director and producer came on the screen, a joint passed from one kid to another. Then a man's voice said, "Pot—Trip or Trap?"

Espie knew the question. She'd seen the film in seventh grade and again during her classes at the police academy, but she didn't know the answer. And when the film ended the kids in the class wouldn't know the answer either, because people who were supposed to know couldn't agree on what the answer was.

The film rolled on, and the kids talked about why they smoked pot, how it made them feel, and what had happened when they'd been busted for using it. Then the experts came on, and the kids around Espie moved impatiently. She didn't blame them. This part of the film was dull—and dumb. One doctor said pot affects the brain but doesn't hurt the body. One said it hurt the body but not the brain. And another one said it hurt the body and the brain. Espie decided maybe the film did give an answer. Pot hurt something, but people couldn't agree what. She'd have to bring that up during class discussions. Her teacher gave grades for participation.

The lights came on, and Bob rewound the film, then put on the other one. The one about marijuana had started without noise. This one almost blasted Espie's ears off. Kids were passing a bottle of beer around and singing. Then the scene changed, and a kid was saying how great he used to be at sports—before he started to drink. There were scenes of his arrest and booking at the police station, then another guy came on, then a girl. She said, "I was at a party and this girl started making margaritas. . . ."

The scene switched to the beach, and the girl's voice came over the roar of the waves. "I can handle getting loaded. I just can't handle coming down."

Espie was waiting for the experts to come on, but they didn't. There were only kids saying, "I didn't know what was going on, and I didn't care as long as I could get my next bottle." "I was shy. I did it to be somebody." "It made me feel better, all right, then my grades went, but I didn't care."

They talked in the past as though they didn't drink anymore. Then the scene switched to kids talking and laughing, and they were drinking cola. A girl sat in front of a cake with a candle on it. She was surrounded by kids. She said, "When you're lonely, talk to somebody about it." She blew out the candle. "This is my first birthday. I've been clean for one year."

The lights came on, and the teacher passed out booklets. "These are from Alcoholics Anonymous. There's a questionnaire about drinking. Read it, and be ready to discuss it tomorrow." The final bell rang, and everybody scrambled.

Espie ran out so Allison wouldn't get away from her. Espie beat her to the car and opened the booklet so Allison could see her reading it. "What's so interesting?" she asked when she came.

She unlocked the doors, and Espie got in. "We saw a film about drinking in Health, and the teacher passed these out. Did you know by the time a kid is thirteen, he's probably had his first taste of liquor?"

Allison started the car. "So?"

"So, I didn't know that."

"When did you have your first drink?" Allison asked as she pulled out into the traffic.

"At twelve. My mother had started hitting the bottle pretty heavy, and I tried it."

"Then you're the same as I am. I took mine at twelve too."

"But you *have* to have booze. I don't."

Allison slowed for a pedestrian. "You don't drink because you don't have the chance. Mrs. Garcia is always around. And you don't have money to buy it."

"If I wanted a bottle, I'd rip it off. I don't drink because I don't *have* to."

"Neither do I. Look, I haven't had a drink since . . ." Allison glanced at Espie. "Since this morning." She said it so softly, Espie hardly heard her.

"This booklet doesn't tell people they shouldn't drink. It says if alcohol gets in the way of school you might have a drinking problem." Espie turned the page. "Hey, here's a test to see if you're an alcoholic or on the way to becoming one. The first question is about school. 'Are you flunking because you miss a lot of classes?' You have to answer yes on that one. The next one asks if you need a drink in the morning."

"Not every morning," Allison said quickly.

"You keep telling me it's hard for you to get going in the morning."

"Because I'm tired."

Espie shrugged. " 'Do you drink alone?' " Allison glanced at her. Espie said, "That's the question."

Allison turned a corner. "Okay, I've got a problem. I've already told you that."

"But you don't always believe it."

Allison stopped the car in front of Espie's house. "I believe it after what happened this weekend," she said. It was funny about eyes. Allison's face looked relaxed. It was her eyes that showed how scared she was.

"Go to an A.A. meeting," Espie said. Allison shook her head. "Then come in and call them. Just talk to them."

"Let me think about it."

Espie opened the door. "Okay. But if you decide to call them, their number is in the phone book." Espie closed the door, and Allison drove away without even a wave.

Espie found a note from Mrs. Garcia telling her to put the spaghetti sauce on the stove at four thirty. She sat down at the kitchen table and started her homework. If she had everything done before Mrs. Garcia got back, she'd be happy, and Espie wanted her that way because she wanted to talk to her about that movie with Rick.

When she came home, Mrs. Garcia put water on the stove to cook the spaghetti and told Espie the doctors had done more tests on Denise. "They say everything is doing the right thing inside. And if Denise works hard on the thera— What is that word?"

"Therapy."

Mrs. Garcia nodded. "If she work hard, she will come home in three or four weeks. She will not walk right, and she will have to go for more therapy"—Mrs. Garcia smiled when she said the word correctly—"but she will be home with us."

"What do you mean she won't walk right? Is she going to be crippled?"

"The doctor say he does not think so, but it will be months from now before she is all better." Mrs. Garcia stirred the spaghetti sauce. "I will not go every day anymore," she said.

"Why?"

"I breathe hard when I see Denise. She is worried about me so she say I should not come so many times. I tell her I still come every day, but she say no. I am afraid she will be sad."

"She'll be okay. The L.E.E.G.s have been going every night, and we'll set up another schedule for them Thursday. And if Carlos gets time off, he'll take us." Espie began to set the table. "I've been worried about you too."

"You have?"

"Well, you haven't been sick all the time I've been here, and now you've had two attacks in a week. It would really be rough on Denise if you got so sick you couldn't go at all."

"You are right. I will go every two days so I can stay well." The water started to boil. Mrs. Garcia put in the spaghetti, and Espie began to pick up her books from the table. Mrs. Garcia said, "I think about Rick and the movie." Espie stopped what she was doing. "I think it is nice you go with him."

Espie realized she was holding her breath. She let it out. "Hey, great."

"But you must go early so you will be home for the curfew at ten o'clock."

"That curfew is for kids who just hang around. The police don't bother anybody if they're on their way home from someplace."

Mrs. Garcia put the dishes on the table. "You must be home at ten o'clock or you cannot go."

Espie didn't want to go on a date at six o'clock, but Mrs. Garcia's voice discouraged arguments. "I'll tell Rick at rehearsal tomorrow," Espie said, and hoped he wouldn't mind going to a six o'clock movie like a couple of kids.

CHAPTER 15

Espie was anxious to tell Allison about Rick the next day, but she wasn't there. If Allison was drinking she wouldn't be able to go to the rehearsal. Espie worried about it all through her classes and hardly paid attention to what was going on, even in her health class, where the discussion was about grass and alcohol.

When classes finally ended, she hurried home to call Allison. The moment Espie opened the door, Mrs. Garcia asked from the kitchen, "You have a nice day in school?"

"Yeah, everything went great, but I have to call Allison. I forgot to ask her what time she was going to pick me up," Espie said.

The phone rang a long time, and the panic Espie had felt all day grew. Mrs. Garcia said, "Maybe she is not home yet."

"She always takes a long time to answer," Espie said, and willed Allison to pick up the phone. When she did, her voice was so soft Espie hardly heard her. "Hi, Allison. I forgot to ask you what time you're coming to pick me up."

"When did I talk to you?" Allison asked, obviously con-

131

fused. Espie couldn't answer that without having to explain to Mrs. Garcia that Allison hadn't been in school. "Sure, six o'clock is okay," she said.

"I'll be there," Allison said, and hung up. She didn't sound like she was in any condition to drive, but Espie didn't care as long as she got to rehearsal to see Rick. She put down the phone, but the panic didn't leave her. You couldn't depend on a drunk.

Espie worried while she did her homework and while she ate. And when she changed her clothes, she wondered if she wasn't getting ready for nothing. At a quarter to six, she went to the living room, and every time she heard a car come down the street she prayed it would be Allison, but none of them even slowed down. But just before six, Espie heard a car stop at the same moment she heard a horn. She ran out and opened the car door. "You're early."

"I haven't seen Joaquin since Friday," Allison said, as though that explained everything. She offered Espie some mints.

Espie took one and put it in her mouth. "What happened to you this morning?"

"Some guy hit me when I was coming down the hill this morning. His car slammed mine against the rail on the side of the road, and I thought I was going into the ravine. It scared the hell out of me. So I went back home for a drink to settle my nerves." She shrugged. "One thing led to another."

She turned a corner and almost hit a car coming the other way. Espie was thrown against the door when Allison straightened out the Firebird. "Hey, watch it," she said. She remembered how Allison had crossed to the other side of the road the day they came down the hill from her house. She'd probably done the same thing this morning.

"What did your mother say about the accident?"

"She doesn't know about it yet. She had a couple of meetings, then she met my father downtown for dinner. They're going to the Music Center tonight."

"The guy's insurance going to pay to fix your car?"

"I don't know. He says the accident was my fault. My father will have to talk to him."

Allison stopped the car behind Joaquin's van. Espie said, "You're just in time to help Joaquin."

Allison hopped out of the car, and Espie followed her. "Need a hand?" Allison asked.

Joaquin grinned. "Sometimes I think I should have taken up the harmonica."

He nodded toward the Firebird. "What happened to your fender?"

"Some guy hit it this morning."

"He going to pay for it?"

"He sure is. It was his fault," Allison told him, and took the two small drums Joaquin handed her.

He picked up the bass and said to Espie, "Grab the cymbals, will you, Espie?" She took them and headed for the hall with Allison and Joaquin behind her. She went up the steps, pushed the door, and held it open for them.

Allison took one step past her and fell. The drums crashed to the floor, and one of them rolled across the room. "You tripped me," Allison screamed at Espie.

"I didn't touch you."

The kids came running. Rick was the first one to reach Allison. "You okay?"

She sat on the floor and rubbed her knee. "She tripped me," Allison repeated.

133

Espie said, "She's crazy."

Joaquin put down his drum and bent down beside Allison. "Are you hurt?"

Allison said, "No, I'm okay." She looked past the kids at the drums she had dropped and began to giggle.

Espie said to Rick, "I guess she tripped on that last step." Allison was still giggling.

Georgie said, "Hey, Allison, what are you on?"

Allison glared at him and struggled to her feet. "Are the drums okay?" she asked Joaquin.

He tapped the one close to him. "This one's okay," he said, and went to get the other one. Allison picked up the bass Joaquin had been carrying and ignored the kids who asked if she was all right.

Rick whispered to Espie, "Is she high on something?"

"She seemed okay on the way over here."

Rick shrugged. "What did Mrs. Garcia say about the movie?"

"I can go as long as I'm home by ten o'clock."

"Ten o'clock?"

"Yeah, she's hung-up on curfew."

He looked disappointed. "Nobody pays attention to that." He smiled. "I don't care. As long as I can be with you."

"That's the way I feel," Espie told him.

Joaquin said, "Hey, Espie, bring the cymbals over here, will you?"

Allison was standing near him. She told Espie, "I'm sorry I yelled at you. I guess I tripped."

Espie ignored her and gave Joaquin the cymbals. Rick said, "Okay, everybody in place," and Espie went to stand beside him. It was becoming a nice habit.

Every so often, she glanced at Allison and found

Joaquin doing the same thing. At the break, Rick said, "There's a good movie at the Highland. Want to go there?"

Espie had heard the kids talk about it in one of her classes. "Yeah, great."

She saw Joaquin hurry toward them instead of staying alone with Allison the way he had done the other nights. Rick asked him, "Have you seen the movie at the Highland?"

Joaquin shook his head. "I might go this weekend. I hear it's great."

Allison had come up behind him. "I'd like to see it," she told him.

Joaquin said, "I'm not really sure I can go. I have a bunch of stuff to do." Espie heard somebody banging the drums. Joaquin said, "Hey, Georgie, want me to show you how to do that?" he asked, and hurried away. Allison followed him, but he didn't even look at her while he concentrated on helping Georgie.

When Rick called the end of the break and told the kids what version of the "Our Father" they were going to sing Sunday, they moaned. Georgie said, "That's too slow."

Rick said, "It sounds religious, and people like it."

Georgie said, "The old ladies like it."

Rick ignored him and played the introduction. The kids were still complaining, but when he gave the signal they began to sing.

They messed up on the second line and had to do it over and over again. The tune was slow and hard to sing, and Espie didn't like it. But if singing it meant Rick could come to the house to teach it to her and to Mrs. Garcia, Espie didn't care what it sounded like.

After rehearsal, Rick held her hand while they walked

135

to the car. Allison stayed behind with Joaquin. But just as Espie and Rick reached the car, Allison hurried past them. "Let's go," she said. Her voice was low and angry.

Rick asked, "What's the matter with you?"

Allison opened the car door. "Ask your friend," she said. She looked at Espie. "You coming, or you going to stand there all night?"

Espie wanted to tell her to go to hell. Instead, she kissed Rick. "I'll see you tomorrow night," she told him, and got in the Firebird.

The moment she closed the door, Allison took off. "Joaquin acted like I had some kind of disease or something."

"Maybe he doesn't like his girls falling all over the floor."

"Everybody trips."

"But they don't act the way you did."

"How would you have acted with everybody looking at you?"

"I don't know, but I wouldn't have yelled at my friend."

"I told you I was sorry about that."

"Look, go to A.A. That booklet on alcoholics could have been written for you. You're flunking, you don't have any friends, you drink alone, you drink until you pass out. . . ."

"I've got you there. I don't pass out. I quit and take a nap." Allison turned a corner. "Only thing is, this afternoon I quit later than usual. I guess that's why I tripped. But Joaquin didn't have to act the way he did."

"Maybe he doesn't want a drunk for a girl."

"I wasn't drunk. Besides, what does he know? He doesn't even drink."

"Not at all?"

"That's what he told me Friday afternoon before my

136

mother kicked him out." Allison slowed the car when she
reached Espie's house but she didn't stop.

"We going for another ride?"

Allison said, "He's still sore about the way my mother
treated him Friday."

"Your mother's got a problem about people. Joaquin
doesn't. He wouldn't blame you for something she said."

Allison stopped the car. "Then what's wrong with
him?"

"I told you. He saw the way you drink. He saw the
way you acted tonight. That's enough to scare off a lot of
people." Espie glanced out the back window. "Take me
home."

The car moved again. "Aren't you going to help me?"

"I've tried to help you, but you won't do what I tell
you."

"You want me to be with a bunch of drunks."

"Do what you want, but I have to get home. I don't
want Mrs. Garcia mad at me."

Allison pulled into a driveway and turned the car
around. "That man said there's a meeting tomorrow
night?"

"It's in the hospitality room of the recreation center at
Lincoln Park." Allison stopped in front of the house. "Are
you going to go?" Espie asked.

"I don't know if they can help me."

"It won't hurt to give them a try."

"I really acted stupid, didn't I?" Espie nodded. Allison
stared out the window. "Maybe I'll go." She looked at
Espie. "Yeah, maybe I will."

"Great," Espie said, and got out.

But before she closed the door, Allison said, "I'm not
sure."

Espie slammed the door. She started up the walk and

remembered what the man at Alcoholics Anonymous had said. "If this person is a friend of yours, try to get her to come." She opened the car door. "We'll talk about it on the way to school, okay?"

"Okay."

Espie hurried up the steps and unlocked the door. Mrs. Garcia asked, "You have a nice time?"

"We worked hard."

"Rick will come tomorrow to teach us the 'Our Father'?" Espie nodded. "I hope he does not mind."

"He doesn't," Espie said, and hummed the song on the way to her room.